The Divas: India

Also by Victoria Christopher Murray

Diamond

The Divas: India

Victoria Christopher Murray

POCKET BOOKS
New York London Toronto Sydney

Pocket Books
A Division of Simon & Schuster, Inc.
1230 Avenue of the Americas
New York, NY 10020

First Pocket Books trade paperback edition August 2008

POCKET and colophon are registered trademarks of Simon & Schuster, Inc.

For information about special discounts for bulk purchases,
please contact Simon & Schuster Special Sales at 1-800-456-6798
or business@simonandschuster.com.

Designed by Carla Jayne Little

Manufactured in the United States of America

10 9 8 7 6 5 4 3 2 1

Library of Congress Cataloging-in-Publication Data is available.

ISBN-13: 978–1–4165–6349–5
ISBN-10:   1–4165–6349–0

The Divas: India

chapter 1

This world wasn't made for me.

I'm too fat. Too tall. My hair is too curly. And I'm too dark—at least that's what I think when I'm hanging out with my cousin from my mother's side of the family. When I'm with my other cousins, I'm way too light. Being India Morrow is sometimes really horrible.

And this was one of those times.

"Come on, India!" Diamond shouted right in my ear. She grabbed my hand and dragged me—even though I wasn't ready—onto the stage.

I struck the pose like I'd practiced over and over with my BFFs. I tried to smile. Just like I smiled at the Kodak Theatre two weeks ago when we officially became the Divine Divas and won that first contest.

At the Kodak, I wasn't even scared. Even though there were two thousand people there, they were two thousand people I didn't know and who didn't know me. And on that big ole stage, I couldn't even see anybody in the audience.

1

But today was different. All the lights were on and I could see almost every one of the faces in the school auditorium. And what was way, way worse was that they could see me.

I looked to one side and there was Aaliyah. She was like five feet eight inches of solid confidence. And on the other side of me was Diamond, looking all . . . well, looking like Diamond. Looking like the star that she always told us she was. Sometimes I wished I could be just like her. Or like Veronique. Or Aaliyah.

"How y'all doing, Holy Cross Prep!" Veronique waved at the kids in the audience.

They cheered. Clapped their hands. Stomped their feet. Made a roar that rumbled through the room. It sounded just like when the crowd cheered at the stadium where my dad played football. The way those big ole men screamed used to scare me. And even though I was so much older now, I was just as scared being on this stage.

I mean, it was true, I was one of the Divine Divas. And, after winning the city championships for the Glory 2 God gospel talent search, we were on our way to San Francisco to compete in the state championships. But everyone knew I wasn't as cute as Diamond. Or as cool as Veronique. Or as smart as Aaliyah. The only thing these kids knew about me was that I was too fat. And too tall. And way too light. . . .

The music blasted through the auditorium. And even though it didn't sound as good as it did in the Kodak Theatre, we started clapping and stepping just like we'd practiced.

I had to keep talking to myself. Keep begging God to help me not trip. Help me to not really look like a big ole fool.

I concentrated on every move, following behind Veronique. I focused on singing every note, staying in harmony with my friends. And I tried to make myself as small as I could, hoping that no one would look at me and wonder what the heck I was doing on this stage.

"I don't want to go to the club," we all sang, "but I want to dance. . . ."

We grooved to the music, hit all the notes, stepped and kicked and twirled the way we'd done at the Kodak in Hollywood. The kids moved with us, dancing and screaming as if we really were stars.

"Go, Diamond," they yelled.

"Go, Vee," they screamed.

"Go, Aaliyah," they chanted.

No one called my name.

Finally, we held our hands in the air and the music stopped. A second passed, and then it was a mad mess. The kids in the front row rushed the stage before our music teacher, Mrs. Cressna, could even stop them.

For a moment, I almost felt good. But then the kids kinda pushed me to the side to get to my friends.

"You were really great," they said to Diamond.

"I didn't know you could sing like that," they complimented Veronique.

"Are you guys going to be on TV?" they asked Aaliyah.

The way Diamond and Veronique were grinning, I could tell they were loving every moment. Even Aaliyah—who always hated this stuff—seemed to be kinda feeling it today.

The crowd became thick, squeezing me farther and farther away. It wasn't long before I was standing at the back of the stage, just watching, as if I wasn't even part of the group. As if I wasn't even part of the school. There were like twenty, thirty, or forty kids on the stage, but no one noticed me.

"Hey, you were good, India."

I turned around, and it took me a moment to remember this boy's name. He was in my French and math class, and the only reason I noticed him was because he was the only black guy I'd ever seen with such red hair. And he had freckles, just like me.

"Thanks," I said.

"You moved pretty good up there."

"Thanks," was all I said again. I folded my arms and lowered my head, wishing he would go away. I felt bad, but I didn't feel bad enough to want Riley to be talking to me. He was as unpopular as I was.

"I was surprised when I heard that you were one of the Divine Divas."

Now I looked at him. "Why?"

"Well"—he stopped for a moment and grinned—"you don't exactly look the type."

I hadn't been feeling him before, and I really wasn't feeling him now. "What type is that?" I growled, hoping that he wasn't getting ready to say what I thought.

"Well . . . I mean . . ." He looked over at Diamond, Veronique, and Aaliyah. "They look so . . ." Maybe it was the way my face turned red that made him stop. "Well, you know what I mean," he finished.

If I was still in elementary school, I would have beaten him up right there. But at Holy Cross Prep, you got suspended for fighting, so I couldn't do that. And I couldn't just stand there and cry either, even though that was all I wanted to do.

"Hey," Riley called as I walked away. "I didn't mean . . ."

I didn't stay around to hear what he didn't mean. Didn't want to. Didn't need to. I just marched right off the stage, through the aisles that were still filled with kids trying to get to the real divas. When I got to the back of the auditorium, I turned around. Seemed like my BFFs didn't even notice that I was gone.

I was so glad that the special pre-Christmas assembly to

introduce the Divine Divas to the school had been called at the end of the day. We were supposed to sing, and then we were all going to hang out. But it seemed like Diamond and Veronique and Aaliyah had forgotten about that.

After I stopped at my locker, I wandered out of the school, not having any idea where I wanted to go. I wasn't ready to go home. My mother would know something was wrong, and she would just tell me what she always told me—that everything was going to be all right.

At the corner of Centinela, I waited for the light to turn green. And as I waited, I tried not to look at my favorite place in the whole world. But the golden arches were right in front of my face. And I could have sworn they were calling my name.

I had promised myself that I was going to stop eating so much junk food. But I loved hamburgers and French fries the way Diamond loved clothes and fashion magazines. I always felt so much better with a hamburger in my hand. And right now, all I wanted was to feel better.

"I'll just have one," I whispered. "Only a cheeseburger. No fries," I promised myself right before I opened the front door.

But when I got to the counter, I don't know how "I'll have two double cheeseburgers, super-size fries, two apple pies, and a large strawberry shake" came out of my mouth.

It didn't even take a minute before I was sitting at one of those tiny tables all by myself.

After the first bite of my cheeseburger, I felt a little better. But it was hard to feel all the way good when I kept thinking about what had just happened. It was just way embarrassing.

When Diamond first came up with the idea for the Divine Divas, I had been so excited. Not because I could sing all that well, or because I wanted to be a star. But being in the group gave me a chance to hang out with my "best friends forever," and whenever I was with them, I felt good. During rehearsals,

I had the best of times. Even the contest at the Kodak Theatre was fun, especially when my friends loved the jewelry I made for us all to wear. It was all good—until we got back to school and the principal announced that we had won the competition. The Divine Divas were a hit. But I wasn't.

I sighed and reached for my other hamburger, but when I looked down, I couldn't believe that I'd eaten both of the cheeseburgers that fast. And the apple pies and most of the fries were gone, too.

Before I could decide what to do, my Kirk Franklin ring tone played on my cell phone. *I've been down so long, I've been hurt for so long. . . .*

I looked at the screen—it was Aaliyah. Finally my friends had noticed that I was gone. I pressed the power and turned off my phone. I was way too mad to talk, even to Aaliyah. I couldn't believe that they had played me like that.

As I stood at the counter and ordered another hamburger, I wondered if I just wasn't meant to be one of the divas. Not that I wanted to quit. My friends would never forgive me, because the singers had to stay the same throughout the competition and if I dropped out, it was over for the Divine Divas. My BFFs would never speak to me again. And if I didn't have them to hang with every day, I didn't know what I would do.

So quitting was not an option, as my dad always said. But if I was going to keep on being a Divine Diva, I had to do something. I never, ever again wanted to feel as bad as I did today.

chapter 2

"Hey, is Drama Mama home?" Diamond bounced on my bed so hard the canopy shook.

"Would you stop calling my mom that?" I said like I was mad. But I wasn't. Sometimes I even laughed when Diamond called my mom that.

Anyway, today I wasn't mad at anybody. This was one of the first times since we performed in the assembly last week that I really felt great. All of my BFFs had come home with me to check out the new jewelry designs I'd made for us to wear for the second round of the contest in San Francisco.

"Drama Mama is not so bad," Veronique said to me as she sat at my computer. She turned it on and started playing with the keys. "It's way better than what she calls my mother."

We all had to laugh at that. Diamond called Veronique's mother the Queen . . . of Mean! But just like me, Veronique didn't really seem to care. Sometimes I wondered if it was because she knew that was a good name for her mom. Ms. Lena really was mean, and sometimes she even scared me. But I guess she had to live like that—kind of strict because she had to take care of Veronique and her four brothers. I may have only been fifteen, but I knew I'd be way mad and way mean, too, if I had to take care of five children all by myself.

Aaliyah's backpack made such a thump on the floor, it scared me.

"What do you have in there?" Veronique asked.

"What do you think?" Diamond said. "Nothing but books. Books, books, books. That's all she cares about." Diamond put her hands on her hips. "Don't you ever get tired of studying?"

Aaliyah shrugged. "Don't you ever get tired of never seeing an A?"

I tried not to laugh, but my giggles came out anyway. I couldn't believe Aaliyah went there. But I guess Diamond had it coming. She always gave Aaliyah such a hard time about being a good student. I think in a way she was kind of jealous. Not that I blamed Diamond. I mean, who wouldn't be a little jealous of all the As Aaliyah got?

"Whatever, whatever." Diamond flicked her fingers across her shoulder like she was brushing off Aaliyah's words. "Anyway, I didn't come over here for all of that." She rubbed her hands together and grinned at me. "Okay, India. We're waiting."

From the moment I'd told my best friends at lunch about my designs, I'd been excited. Now I wasn't so sure. Suppose they didn't like these new pieces? Suppose they thought that everything I'd made was stupid?

Slowly, I took the black velvet box from my nightstand. But before I could even get it all the way out, Diamond grabbed the box and flipped open the top.

I held my breath as my best friends stared at the silver chains and charms I'd made. A little while ago, I thought my designs were really cool. But the way my BFFs just sat there with their mouths open, I wished I had kept it all to myself.

"These are gorgeous." Aaliyah lifted one of the chains and then jumped up and stood in front of my mirror. Before I knew it, Diamond and Veronique were right behind her doing the same thing with chains they'd pulled from the box.

They were oohing and aahing and giggling so much that finally I remembered to breathe.

"This is the one I want!" Diamond posed in the mirror wearing the triple-strand silver chain that came all the way down to her knees. "This is fierce!"

"Yeah, my sistah." Veronique grinned at me. "I didn't know you had this in you."

"I've got to find something awesome to wear with this." Diamond strutted across my room as if she were a model. "I'm not waiting for San Fran. I'm gonna wear this now. We need to go shopping."

Okay, now see—just when I was starting to feel good, Diamond had to bring up shopping. That's all she ever talked about. I swear, if she had her way, there would be a mall attached to the back of her house.

I hated shopping, especially with my BFFs. I could never wear the same clothes or even shop in the same stores that they did. So whenever we went to the mall, I just walked around with them, carrying their bags and feeling bad.

"Yeah, let's go shopping," Veronique added, making me feel way, way worse. I knew she liked to shop, but Veronique never had any money. And then she said, "I can actually buy something when we hit the mall. My mom said that all the money that I'm making from my job I can keep for the Divine Divas."

"That's great!" The way Diamond cheered, you would have thought Veronique had just won the lottery or something.

"Make sure you save some of that money for San Fran. We're gonna have a couple of days there, and we'll really be able to hang in the stores."

"New York is where I really want to go," Veronique said.

"Of course, the NYC is like triple A when it comes to finding fashion or anything else," Diamond said, as if she was some kind of professor of shopping. "But no worries. Being the fashionista that I am, I know some great places in San Fran, too."

"Yeah, I was there with my dad last year," Aaliyah said. "Union Square is the place to go."

Okay, this was bad. Shopping was definitely Diamond's thing and sometimes Veronique's. But I could always count on Aaliyah to hate shopping as much as I did. I guess being a Divine Diva had changed her, too.

Thinking that we could stay away from the mall, I asked, "Why can't we just have my mom's friend make our clothes like we did last time?"

"Now, you know working with Drama Mama's designers was hot, but that's all the more reason why we need to get to the mall. To scope out some outfits. We *need* to shop to get inspired."

Inspired? What kind of inspiration did we need? "Tova's designers can make us anything we want."

Diamond laughed. "You always crack me up, calling your mom Tova. Shoot," she bounced back on the bed, "if I ever called the judge Elizabeth, my mother would slap me so hard, I wouldn't even need a plane to get to San Fran."

"You know?" Veronique added. We all knew her mother would do the same thing.

I shrugged. Yeah, I called my mother by her first name. That's how she wanted it—from the time I was a little girl. I think it made her feel like she was more my friend than my mother. Sometimes it was cool. But most of the time I just wished that she'd let me call her Mom.

Diamond said, "Let's hit the mall this weekend," getting right back to her favorite topic. "This will be my first weekend off punishment, and I need to get started on my Christmas shopping anyway."

"I'm down," Veronique said. "If I don't have to babysit."

Diamond picked up another one of my chains and wrapped this long one around her waist. "I'm thinking, we need to take this fashion stuff seriously. I mean, we're gonna be huge stars, and maybe soon we'll have our own line of clothes. The Divine Divas line."

"Sounds good, my sistah." Veronique laughed.

"Yeah, Diamond. That's the first good idea you've had," Aaliyah said. "You guys can design the clothes and I'll be the CEO and run everything."

Diamond pinched her lips together and made a face. "You'll be the CEO? I thought you were going to be a nuclear physicist or something."

"I can be both."

While my friends debated about their company that didn't even exist, I sat on the floor, crossed my legs yoga-style, and leaned against the wall. Diamond, Veronique, and Aaliyah didn't even notice that I wasn't primping and posing with them.

Now I was almost sorry that I'd asked them to come over. We were in my house, in my bedroom, and I still felt invisible. It was always like this once the talk turned to clothes and shopping and all the stuff that didn't have a thing to do with me.

Not that I really hated clothes. If I could look as cute as my friends in anything, I'd always want to go shopping, too. Everything looked good in a size five, seven, or nine. But get that same skirt for a big girl, and you had an elephant wearing a tutu.

"Okay, so we're set for this weekend, right?" Diamond asked.

"I have to work Saturday morning, but as long as I don't have to babysit, I'll be free by noon."

"I'm cool, too," Aaliyah said, "but I don't want to be out all day."

"I know, I know," Diamond said, waving Aaliyah's words away before she got to say anything about wanting to study. Then she glanced around my bedroom like she was looking for something. "India, why're you sitting over there? Come here." She held up the first chain she'd tried on. "I have just two questions. Can I have this one for my birthday?" She laughed, but I knew she was serious. "And my second question is, which one are you gonna wear, 'cause we gotta look fierce in San Fran?"

I put on a happy face before I pushed up from my hiding place. I already knew which chain I wanted to wear. What I hadn't figured out was what I was going to wear with my chain. I had made up my mind—I wasn't going to San Francisco as a fat girl.

I hooked my chain around my neck.

"San Fran here we come," Diamond said, and then we all struck a pose in the mirror like we were on the stage. "But first, we gotta go to the mall!"

This time, I laughed with my BFFs. Now all I had to figure out was a way to keep laughing on the outside, and maybe that would help me stop crying on the inside.

chapter 3

There's a reason why Diamond called my mother Drama Mama.

Everything with Tova was so over the top. Like the way we had to sit for dinner—every night. As if we were some big movie-star family or something. I remember when I saw that old movie, *Soul Food,* and they had these big huge dinners. That was cool because it was only on Sunday nights and there were a whole lotta people in that family. But at our house, it was like that every day, even though it was just me, my mom, and my dad.

Not only that, we had to eat at the dining table, not the one in the kitchen. The big ole one in the dining room that was made of mahogany or something. And we had to be dressed. Not like fancy dressed, but Tova wouldn't let me (or my dad) wear any kind of jeans. I wondered if that's how they did things in Sweden, where my mother was from. But I didn't know. My mother never talked a lot about when she grew up.

But even though my mom didn't talk about that, there were lots of other things that Tova talked about. Like how she used to be a high-fashion model. She could talk about that all day and all night.

Not that I wasn't proud—I was really glad that Tova was my mom. Looking at all the old pictures of her when she was modeling in all kinds of foreign countries was way cool. Even when she was my age, my mom was beautiful. And even though she was kind of old now, I thought she was still as pretty as any of the models who were in all those magazines. That's why I could never figure out how she ended up with a daughter like me.

"So, how was practice today?" my dad asked, right when I put a big ole chunk of meat loaf in my mouth.

"It was good," I said after I swallowed my food.

He frowned. "I thought you'd be more excited. You're not looking forward to San Francisco?"

"I am," I lied. But it wasn't a total lie. I did have some good feelings about hanging out with my best friends. It was just this fat thing that made me all crazy.

"Well, I have something."

I was glad my mother was changing the subject, because my dad could usually figure out when something was wrong with me, and I didn't want him to ask me any more questions.

"A big surprise." My mother pushed her chair back from the table, and then spread her arms open real wide, like she was going to say something major.

When my dad rolled his eyes, I couldn't help but laugh. Straight drama—that's what my mom was all about.

My dad and I already knew what Tova was going to say. Maybe not the exact words, but she was going to tell us something about some charity program she'd been invited to host. Or some special event she had to attend. My mom did a lot of stuff like that in the community. It was all good—as long as she didn't drag me along with her.

Not that I didn't like hanging with Tova, especially when

we just stayed home and watched TV together. Or when she hung out in my room and helped me design my jewelry. My mom was way cool like that.

But whenever she wanted to take me out—that was the part I couldn't get with. Being in public with my mom was H-A-R-D. Everyone was always falling all over her and telling her how pretty she was. And then they would almost faint when she introduced me as her daughter.

"Marvin," my mom called out to my dad when she saw him rolling his eyes, "are you making fun of me?"

She sounded like she was mad, but I knew she wasn't. My father always made faces like that when my mom started acting over the top. It was just his way of teasing her.

"Sweetheart," my dad started to say. And then he gave her those puppy-dog eyes. "I would never make fun of you." The way he looked at her, like he was all sad, made me crack up even more.

Even Tova had to laugh. "Comedian!" But then she waved her hand in the air like she didn't care what my father said. "Are you both ready to hear my news?"

"Yes, darling," my father said in his sweetest voice.

But he wasn't pretending this time. He had that look in his eyes that sometimes embarrassed me. Even though my mother and father had been married forever, they were still always hugging and kissing all over each other. And not just at home. They would even do that stuff in public so other people could see. How embarrassing was that?

"*This City Paris* magazine is coming to interview me on Saturday! And they want to take pictures of you." She pointed to my father. Then it got way, way worse. She turned to me. "And you too, honey."

I almost choked on my meat loaf. But before I could say anything, my father came to my rescue.

"Another magazine? My goodness, Tova, you're not even modeling anymore. Why all these interviews?"

"Because I'm *not* modeling anymore. And I have to stay relevant. A lot of older models are getting gigs these days, and if I keep my name out there, something wonderful may come up for me."

Okay, now see—dinner had been just regular and we'd been having fun. But there wasn't anything funny about this. Pictures in a magazine? I mean, yeah, Tova took great pictures. That was way obvious. But do you know what I looked like standing next to her? That elephant in a tutu . . .

"I'm not gonna do it!" I said.

There was no way. Not after what happened the last time. It was for a Mother's Day special issue. That magazine wanted photos of celebrity moms and their daughters. The photographer took pictures of me and Tova for an hour, and just when I started to feel okay, he asked me if I felt lucky to have Tova as my stepmother. As if someone as beautiful as Tova couldn't possibly have a real daughter as ugly as me. I just wanted to die right there.

"No." I shook my head at Tova and at that horrible memory.

My mother reached across the table and put her hand on top of mine. "Honey, you can't say no. And anyway, you need to get used to doing these interviews. You're a star now, and soon your dad and I will be joining you on photo shoots for the Divine Divas."

This was getting really bad. Nobody had said a thing to me about magazines wanting to take pictures of me and my friends. I could dance a little, and sing a lot. But taking pictures next to my BFFs? Nuh-huh. That was almost as bad as standing next to Tova.

"My little magazine interviews will be good training for you," Tova said.

I didn't need any training. What I needed was some more mashed potatoes. With the way my mom cooked them, soaking the potatoes in garlic for hours and then adding cheese after they were cooked, I knew that if I had a little bit more with another little slice of meat loaf, I would feel much better about all of this.

But as soon as I reached for the big spoon, my mother grabbed my hand. "Honey, we'll be doing the interview in just a couple of days."

Okay . . . so what did that have to do with garlic-cheese mashed potatoes right now?

Then Tova broke it down for me. "Remember the equation?"

My face got fire hot, and slowly I pulled my hand away. Of course I remembered the equation. How could I forget it—a moment of pleasure on the lips equals a lifetime of inches on the hips. My mother taught me that before I even knew what hips were.

But why did Tova have to say that to me now? I was already feeling bad. I just wanted a little bit more to eat so that I could feel better. Even though it was just my mom and dad sitting there, I was still way embarrassed. No matter who was around, I was humiliated every time she said that to me.

I could feel the tears coming, but I pushed hard not to cry. 'Cause if I did, then Tova would feel bad, and my dad would try to hug me. And none of that would make a difference anyway.

"I have to finish my homework."

"Honey . . ." The way my mother said that, I could tell she felt bad about what she'd said. But it was way too late for sorry.

"I have to write a paper for English class," I said, not even letting my mother talk.

"Go on, honey," my father said. He knew that Tova had hurt my feelings. "I'll help your mother clean up."

I couldn't wait to get away from that table. But even as I ran down the hallway, I heard my father say, "I told you to stop saying that to her."

There was no way I wanted to hear them fight, so I closed my bedroom door right away. My mom and dad never fought—except when it came to me.

I went straight to my closet, but before I slid open the door, I stopped. I had promised myself I wouldn't do that anymore. Promised myself that I was going to get rid of that box.

So I just lay on my bed and tried to block out every word my mother had said and tried to forget about all the good stuff just waiting for me in my closet.

Why did we have to do interviews? Why did I have to take pictures? Why did I have to be so fat? Why couldn't I just look like my mother? Or my best friends?

I couldn't keep my eyes away from my closet, but every time I looked over there, I shook my head. I meant it this time. I was going to do better. I just had to do what Tova always told me to do and have a little willpower—whatever that was.

"No, Tova!" I cringed when I heard my dad's voice. He wasn't really yelling, but I could tell that he was upset.

I got up and opened my door a little so that I could hear. It sounded like my parents had left the dining room and were now headed toward their bedroom.

I waited until I heard their door close, then I tiptoed down the hall to my spot, next to the linen closet. My parents didn't know that if you opened that door, anyone could hear anything going on in their bedroom.

"Marvin, keep your voice down," my mother said.

"Okay. I'm sorry, but I'm not going to let you take India

to any doctor. My goodness, Tova, she's only fifteen. I'm not gonna let anyone cut on my daughter."

"It's not like that, Marvin. So many people are having that surgery—"

"If they're obese!"

Obese? Did Tova think I was obese?

I wanted to run back to my room, but I just had to listen even though they were having the same argument about me. My parents were always fighting about that stomach operation that wouldn't make me fat anymore.

When I first heard my mom talk about it last year, it scared me, 'cause I wasn't trying to be in nobody's hospital. But I was starting to feel kinda different now. I mean, if a doctor could take away my fat, then I needed to do it. Anything to make my fat and their fights go away.

"You don't have to be obese to have the operation. Look, let me just take India in for a consultation. And then we can decide."

"No, Tova. India is fine. She's beautiful, she's smart, she's—"

"She's all of that. But she's not confident. And it's confidence and self-esteem that I want to give her."

"You can't get that through surgery, Tova. No, any kind of surgery is out!"

As my father's voice got louder, my heart pounded harder. By the time I tiptoed back to my bedroom, I couldn't do anything to stop my tears.

It scared me whenever my mom and dad argued. In our house, what my dad said was the law, but whenever they were arguing about this fat operation, my mother wouldn't back down. So I was always afraid that a fight could lead to a divorce and it would all be because of me.

Now I needed my stash real bad. My mouth already started

to water as I slid the glass door open and grabbed the shoe box from the top shelf.

Sitting on my bed, I counted everything that I had packed inside. I had filled it up just a couple of days ago with six Twinkies, three cupcakes, and two slices of lemon cake.

"I'll just have one," I promised myself. Just one cupcake would help me to stop thinking about my parents' fight. Or the magazine interview.

I unwrapped the cellophane slowly, but then I ate the cupcake fast, like I was starving. I was finished before I could even taste it. I needed a little more.

I took out one Twinkie and one slice of cake. That would make it one of each. I dumped the box over the side of my bed, then I leaned back so that I could eat until I felt better.

"Many people are having the surgery. . . ." and *"If they're obese . . ."* and *"I wanna give her confidence,"* and *"I'm not going to allow it."*

All the words my parents said kept coming to my mind. Did my mother really think I was obese? Why did my dad want to stop me from having the surgery if it would help?

I couldn't stand those voices in my head anymore and clicked on my TV. Lying across my bed, I ate another Twinkie. I flipped through the channels. And ate another cupcake.

On the Home and Garden Channel, some lady was making jewelry out of everyday household items. I watched. And I ate until I felt better.

The only thing was, I felt better in my head, but not in my stomach. My stomach hurt so much that I didn't even feel better in my head anymore.

I reached for my stash box, and when I lifted it up, I couldn't believe it. It was empty—except for all the wrappers and papers. I had eaten all of that without even knowing it. And now I felt worse than when I started.

"Honey!" It sounded like Tova was right outside my bed-room.

Even though I was really hurting, I jumped up and stuffed the box under my bed right before my mother came in.

"Honey, did you finish your report?"

I nodded, because I felt too sick to talk and I didn't want to lie out loud.

"Come here." Tova took my hand and sat down on the bed. She turned off the TV with the remote before she said, "I'm sorry if I made you feel bad at dinner."

I shrugged. "I didn't feel bad."

"I didn't mean to hurt your feelings, India. I just want the best for you," she said, stroking her hands through the curls in my hair. "I want you to be all that you can be. I want you to look absolutely fabulous."

I looked at my mother. With her blond hair swept up into a French roll. With her skin looking so smooth and soft even though she didn't have on any makeup. With her body looking like she was still a model. How would I *ever* look fabulous like her?

Then she said, "But what's even more important than looking fabulous is feeling fabulous. That's what I want for you."

And I blurted out, without thinking, "Then why can't I have the surgery?"

My mother frowned.

Uh-oh, I shouldn't have said that. Suppose she figured out that I had a secret listening hiding place?

"Were you listening to—"

"No," I said before she could finish. "I just heard a little. But not just today. I heard you and Daddy talking about it before."

The way Tova nodded, real slow, and the way her eyes were

down, I knew she was sad. "Honey, your dad doesn't think the surgery is a good idea."

I twisted on my bed and faced her. "But maybe I could have it and we wouldn't have to tell him."

My mom smiled a little. "Now, would you really want to do that? Would you really want to lie to your father that way?"

Yeah, I would lie to the world to get skinny! But I didn't say that out loud.

"We're not going to do that. We're just going to find a way to help you eat healthier, okay?"

I nodded, although I knew that wouldn't work. I'd been trying to eat healthy all my life. But healthy food never made me feel any better. And it didn't taste as good.

She smiled and then hugged me. "You're going to be fine, honey. I promise." When she pulled back, she added, "Why don't you come downstairs and help me unpack the Christmas decorations. We're going to put up the tree this weekend."

My stomach was still doing somersaults. I shook my head. "I'm not feeling well. I'm gonna go to bed."

Tova frowned. She held her hand to my head. "You don't have a fever."

"It's not that kind of sick."

My mom nodded, like she knew exactly what I meant.

"Okay, then, get some rest. I'll see you in the morning." She kissed my cheek. "You know I love you, right?" But it was one of those rhetorical questions that I'd learned about in English, because she didn't wait for me to answer. She just left me alone.

Most of the time I guessed I thought that Tova loved me. But it wasn't enough, because God hadn't made me so that I could love myself.

chapter 4

I used to always like school.

It was the one place where I could hang out with my best friends and not feel so different.

But not anymore.

I could hardly find a place at the table where we always ate our lunch together. It used to be just me, Diamond, Veronique, and Aaliyah. But now it seemed like everyone in the whole tenth grade wanted to sit with us.

"Squeeze in here next to me," Aaliyah said when she saw me standing at the end of the table.

When I put my tray down, I wanted to die right there. Why did I have to order three hamburgers and extra fries today? Everyone was staring at my plate like I was a pig or something.

"So, when are you guys going to be on TV?" one of the boys asked.

I didn't even know the names of half the people sitting with us.

"Soon," Diamond said.

"For real?" This time, it was one of the girls who piped in.

"Yeah, I'm sure they're going to put us on TV," Diamond bragged. "Especially after we win the whole competition. You know, we'll get a record contract then."

"Wow," everyone said.

Diamond smiled as if she was already a star. And Veronique was grinning wide. I expected that from them, but what was way worse was that Aaliyah was laughing, too.

Although Diamond and Veronique were my best friends, I was way, way close to Aaliyah. I told her everything, and sometimes it really did feel like we were sisters. That was why I called Aaliyah my bestest of the best. And right now, my bestest wasn't supposed to be acting this way. But it looked like Aaliyah was as caught up as Diamond and Veronique.

While they kept talking about how we were going to San Francisco and then to New York, I just kept eating. It wasn't like I was being antisocial or anything. I wanted to talk, but no one talked to me.

"You're excited, too, right, India?" Aaliyah asked.

I just shrugged. Even though I could tell that she was trying to bring me into the conversation, I was mad at her. Why couldn't she hate all this stuff like she used to? Like I did?

"Well, I think y'all are all hot," another boy said. "Especially you, Vee."

"Really?" Veronique's eyes got all big.

Okay, now see—this was really going way off. Veronique was sitting there, giggling and looking up at that boy like she was Diamond. I laughed but then stopped quick when I caught the frown on Diamond's face.

Uh-oh. It didn't take a big brain to figure this out. Diamond was used to being the star. And the way she was frowning and huffing and puffing, I knew trouble was coming.

When I stood up and slipped away from the table, not

one of my best friends seemed to notice. Things had surely changed since we'd become the divas.

I dumped my tray on the conveyer belt, grabbed my bag, and didn't bother to say good-bye. I felt like I weighed five hundred pounds when I dragged out of the cafeteria.

"India, wait up."

Riley, who was sitting at one of the tables in the back of the room, waved at me. I spun around like I was running track or something and got out of there. I wasn't about to wait and have him insult me like he did the other day.

I dashed into the hallway and then the bathroom. This would be my hideout for a little while. Two girls followed me in, but they didn't say a word to me—not even a little hello. They just kept on talking as if I wasn't even there.

"That's really cool," one of the girls said to the other as they glanced in the mirror and smeared more gloss on their lips. "I wish I'd heard about that contest first. We could have started our own group."

"You know?" the other girl said. She smacked her lips, then grabbed her books. "Maybe we should talk to Diamond or Veronique. Maybe they wouldn't mind expanding the group."

"They *really* should think about adding us to the group. We could bring extra-special flava to the Divine Divas."

They laughed, then walked right past me.

And as I stood in that bathroom alone, I wondered how anybody so fat could be so invisible.

chapter 5

There was only one good thing about this interview.

It was Saturday and that meant that since I had to do this with Tova and my dad, I couldn't go to the mall with my best friends.

I was praying that maybe this interview wouldn't be so bad, since this time my dad was going to be there. No one would say anything mean with the ex star defensive lineman for the Oakland Raiders sitting right next to me.

Looking in the mirror, I didn't feel so bad today. It had to be because of my bestest friend. Yesterday after school, Aaliyah had come over and helped me get ready for this.

"First of all," she'd said, "you need to wear your hair different. Let's try it up."

As I'd sat on the bed, Aaliyah had grabbed a brush and a handful of my hair.

"But I don't like my hair off my face." I'd known I'd been whining, but I hadn't been able to help it. I always wore my hair down, over my ears and way over my fat cheeks.

26

"India, you have such a pretty face, and it's about time that you let the world see it."

That's what everyone always said—that I had a pretty face. That was code for: you're fat, so that's the only nice thing I can say about you. I'd known that's not what my bestest had meant, so I'd let it slide.

Aaliyah had kept brushing, but I still hadn't been convinced until she'd swept my hair up and twisted it at the top. It had looked kinda cute. And then she'd put a little blush on my cheeks—that had made them seem smaller. And with that berry lip gloss, my mouth had looked fuller, better. Even I'd had to smile when I'd looked in the mirror.

"See, I told you. You look gorgeous."

She'd been exaggerating, because gorgeous wasn't the word I would have used. But I had looked better than I'd thought I would.

Next she'd helped me pick out my clothes.

"Do you have one of these skirts in every color?" Aaliyah had laughed.

I'd laughed with her. I did love my peasant skirts because I didn't look so fat in them. And they were long, too—hid my legs.

"I think you should do this one." Aaliyah had held up the light blue skirt. "You said this is for a spring issue, right?"

I'd nodded.

"Well, this is a good spring color and goes great with your eyes." Then she'd picked out a green and blue top that tied at the neck.

By the time my bestest had gone home last night, I'd been feeling good.

Now, as I was getting ready for the interview, I still had that good feeling. Tova was going to be proud. She would like my hair up. And she was always trying to get me to wear a little bit of makeup, so I put on blush and gloss like Aaliyah had shown me.

"Honey," my mother called. "Are you almost ready?"

"Uh-huh." I couldn't wait for her to see me. I turned around right when Tova walked into my room. I faced her. And then I frowned. Just like my mother was frowning at me.

"Oh, honey, you *cannot* wear that."

Okay, now see—that good feeling was starting to go away.

Tova was already in my closet, searching before I could say anything. "It's not true that big clothes are good if you're a little overweight. All big clothes do is make you look big," my mother said as she pushed hangers from one side of the closet to the other. "We have to find something more slimming."

I just stood there, letting her go on and on.

"You're almost sixteen." Tova kept talking, as if I needed to hear this. "You have to think about these things. I want you to always look your best."

What about feeling my best? But I guess my feelings didn't matter—especially since Tova had come in here and wiped all my good feelings away.

It must've been the look on my face that made Tova stop her fat girl lecture for a moment. "Oh, honey." She paused and hugged me. "I know this is hard, sweetheart, and I wish I could help you more." She shook her head and went right back to my closet. "I wish your father would reconsider the operation."

I wished that she would stop saying that, since it was never going to happen.

"Now, this is perfect!"

I gagged at the black pantsuit Tova held up. I looked terrible in that! Not only was it black and made me look like an old lady but it also didn't even fit me right anymore.

"Tova, that jacket is tight on me."

"Oh, you'll be fine," my mother said, holding the clothes up to the light of the window to get a better look. "I always liked you in this suit." She handed the hanger to me. "You'll look fabulous."

No, I won't, was what I wanted to say, but it wouldn't have done any good. Whenever Tova got an idea, she was like a bulldozer. Not even my father could stop her.

The doorbell rang, and my mother glanced out the window. "Okay, they're here," she said, starting to talk fast. That's how she got when she was excited. "Now, hurry up, honey." She rushed toward my door. "This is going to be so good. Our first European magazine together. Aren't you excited?" Another one of her rhetorical questions. Then she said, "By the way, your hair looks fantastic!"

She was gone before I could say anything. All I could do was slip off the perfect outfit that Aaliyah and I had picked out. And put on that ugly you-need-to-be-one-hundred-years-old-to-wear-this suit. As I got dressed, I wondered if my mother was doing this on purpose. Maybe she wanted me to look bad so that she would look good. But it didn't take me a second to change my mind. How stupid was that? My mother didn't need me to look good.

Tova was just being Tova.

And I would just be who I was. The fat fifteen-year-old girl who hated her life.

Sometimes I felt like two different people.

Like right now, I was really embarrassed, wearing this pant-suit. But the moment I walked into the living room, I felt different. It was weird—it was like having a good feeling and a bad feeling at the same time.

That good feeling: I felt proud. Just looking at my mother

and father standing together. If my dad hadn't been a football player, he could have been a model, too. Well, maybe not like a real model, since he was so big. But my daddy was really handsome to me. And to my friends—Diamond was always talking about how fine my father was.

Tova and my dad really looked good together, even though they were total opposites. Daddy's skin was dark and smooth like a big ole piece of Hershey's chocolate. And Tova's looked like pink sponge cake. Daddy had all these big muscles. Tova was long and lean—that's how Diamond described her.

I had read all the magazine articles that talked about my mom and dad when they were dating and then got married. Everyone called them Beauty and the Brawn.

That always made me wonder—what would the magazines call me if they had to come up with a name for the Beauty and the Brawn's daughter? Just thinking about that made me stop feeling proud. Made me think about my pantsuit and get that embarrassed/bad feeling all over again.

"Oh, here she is." My mother was talking in that voice that sounded like she was about to start singing. Then she swooped over to me like she was in some kind of movie. Straight drama!

"This is our daughter, India."

"India, that's a lovely name."

I wondered if the lady who'd said that was a model, too. She looked like one.

"Hello, I'm Nicolette. I'll be interviewing you and your parents today."

I shook her hand, tried to smile. And hoped that she wasn't looking at the way the buttons were almost popping off my jacket.

"So, your name is India," she said with a French accent that I loved. "A beautiful name for a beautiful girl."

I waited for her to just bust out laughing, because I knew she meant that as a joke. But all she did was smile at me, and I smiled back. Okay, now see—maybe this wasn't going to be so bad.

There were two guys in the living room, too, but they didn't say a word. They were busy setting up lights and cameras.

"Why don't we all sit here?" Tova was talking as if she had just come up with that idea. But last night, she'd told my dad and me exactly how this interview was going to go down. She told us where we were going to sit, how she was going to talk first, and then my dad.

Just like my mom had told me to do last night, I sat down between the two of them and held my breath, because I was afraid that if I breathed, a button would pop off. And then I would just have to die right there.

"Okay, let's get started," Nicolette said. "Tova, you are still one of the most beautiful women on the planet."

I grinned. I was having that proud feeling again.

Nicolette asked, "How do you stay in such wonderful shape?"

"Well, you know what I've always said—by any means necessary." And then my mother laughed. But it wasn't one of her regular laughs. She was acting like a movie star again.

"Marvin, you must be really proud of her." Nicolette turned to my father.

"I am. In fact"—he stopped and took my hand—"I'm proud of both of my girls."

Okay, now see—that good feeling was getting way bigger.

"Tova, you know, there is great controversy these days about models being too thin. How do you feel about that?"

"Well, I've always agreed with the cliché that is famous in our business—you can never be too thin or too beautiful."

31

"So, you don't think that some models are dangerously thin?"

"No. Sometimes it's genetics. A woman can't help it if she was born to be a size zero."

A size zero? How was that even possible? My cousin Jill wore a size two, and that was about as little as I thought you could get.

Nicolette said, "But not everyone who wears a zero was born to be that way. You've got to be aware of the drastic measures that women and even some guys have been taking."

"You must be talking about eating disorders."

"Yes. Did you ever experience any of those challenges while you were actively modeling?"

I frowned. I had never heard these kinds of questions before. I thought this was going to be the same ole interview—how did my mother spend her days? What kind of charity work did she do? That kind of stuff. But this Nicolette lady was different.

Tova lowered her voice a little. "Well, in my earlier years, we had to do whatever it took to stay in the clothes. The designers in my day were not playing. We had to appeal to them. Of course, now that I'm older I know diet and exercise are best. But as international models, most of us didn't have two hours to spare at the gym."

"So, you don't have any eating disorders now?"

Uh-oh. The way my mother looked at Nicolette, for a minute I thought she was about to get up and slap her or something. But then, in an instant, that movie-star smile was back. "Of course not. And please make a note that I've never actually said that I had an eating disorder."

Nicolette smiled. "Duly noted. I'm asking these questions because one of the messages I want to get out with this series of articles on models is that the impossible standards that we set up are killing our children. Even five-year-old girls are try-ing to diet.

"So, I'm glad to hear your views on the lessons you've learned about eating and exercise." Nicolette looked at her notes and turned to me. "India, how do you feel about your mother's success?"

Before I could answer, Tova said, "Our daughter is a star in her own right. She is one of the Divine Divas. If you haven't yet heard about them, you will soon."

I didn't get to say a word as Tova—and my dad—told Nico-lette all about my best friends and me forming the group and winning the first contest.

"That's absolutely terrific. This is a family full of stars," Ni-colette said.

I was starting to really like this lady. If my mother ever wanted to do an interview again, I wouldn't mind—as long as Nicolette was doing it.

"Okay, well, let's take some pictures," Nicolette told the cameramen. "Let's do a couple of family photos first."

This was the part that I had dreaded since Tova made the big announcement on Wednesday. But it wasn't so bad—especially with my dad there. With every picture, he held my hand or put his arm around my shoulders.

After about fifty poses, Nicolette said, "Okay, Tova, are you ready to do your thing?"

My dad and I stood off to the side while my mom became the star. I had nothing but good feelings watching her. She was so beautiful in that green dress, and it made me think that my peasant skirt would have been perfect next to her. But at least this was all over. And I hadn't lost one button off my suit.

"Now, India, I'd like to get some pictures of just you."

What! That's what I screamed inside.

"That's a wonderful idea, Nicolette," Tova said. "Thank you so much."

Tova must not have seen the look on my face—I just wanted to die, right here, right now.

"Stand over here," Tova said in that bulldozer tone that let me know nothing was going to get me out of this.

"Daddy!" I whispered to my father, hoping that he could do something.

But it seemed like he knew Tova was in bulldozer mode, too. "Go on, honey," he whispered back. "It'll be all right."

It took me a long time to walk over to the window where my mother stood. "Here, let me fix your makeup for you." Tova grabbed her case off the table and brushed my cheeks. Then she handed me a tube of gloss and I spread the gel over my lips. At least if I had died right then, I would have looked good when I got to heaven.

"Loosen up," Nicolette said when they began to take the pictures.

How was I supposed to do that when I had that elephant-in-a-tutu feeling again? Nicolette kept telling me what to do, how to stand, where to put my hands. I just kept breathing and tried not to die.

It felt like ten hours had passed when Nicolette finally said, "Okay, this will be the last one."

The camera flashed. And I breathed. Finally. Still alive.

"You know, India," Nicolette began, "you're a natural. I can truly see you following in your mother's footsteps."

I waited for her to laugh. She didn't. I was liking this lady even more than I did before.

"When you lose all of that baby fat, I think you're going to be a real beauty."

It was like the whole room froze. Even the cameramen stopped moving. I just stared at this lady who, just a little while ago, had looked so pretty to me, who spoke with that beautiful accent, and who had been so nice.

How could she be so mean now?

I never wanted to cry in front of anyone. That's why I had to run out of the room, because I could feel the tears busting through my eyes.

"I'm sorry," I heard the French lady say. "I didn't mean anything. I was just . . ." I slammed my bedroom door before I could hear her say anything more.

I bounced on my bed, but before I could get a good cry in, my dad was right in the room with me.

"Sweetheart," he said. "Nicolette didn't mean anything—"

"Daddy," I cried. "She called me fat!"

He sat down on the bed and put his arms around me. My dad always made me feel like a big ole teddy bear was hugging me. But even though he held me tight, this time he couldn't make me feel any better.

"She's really sorry, but that's not what she meant. She was just saying . . ." And then he stopped. Like he knew that he couldn't say anything to make the bad feelings go away.

So he just held me. And tried to make me feel better with his arms. And while he did that, I cried, just a little. But not for long. Because I didn't want to think about how bad I felt. All I wanted to think about was how I was going to fix this. What was I going to do to make sure that no one ever called me fat again?

chapter 6

I flipped my cell phone closed. "That was Sybil," I said. "She's running late and wants us to get started. She said she'll be here in about twenty minutes."

"Well, we can't start a thing without Vee." Aaliyah paused and looked at her watch. "And she needs to come on, because I need to get out of here on time tonight."

Diamond rolled her eyes.

"And not to study, Ms. Dee." Aaliyah folded her arms and stared Diamond down. "My dad's taking me Christmas shopping."

"I thought we were all going shopping together on Saturday."

"We are," Aaliyah told Diamond. "But I have to go out at least one day with my dad to get gifts for my grandma and my aunts and uncles—you know the deal. And whenever we do this, I always get to pick up a couple of things for me, too."

"That's cool. The judge told me she wanted us to go shopping, too, but she's been kinda busy with a case." The way Diamond paused and bit her lip, I knew there was more. "Before Vee and Sybil get here, I want to ask you guys something." She stopped again, and this time she spoke with a lower voice. I knew trouble was coming. "How do y'all feel about Vee having the lead all the time?"

Aaliyah didn't even let a second pass. "That's the way it should be. She's the best singer."

"No, she's not," Diamond said. "You are."

"I'm not, but even if I was, I don't want to be the lead. How many times do I have to tell you that?"

Diamond looked at me, and I shook my head. "I don't want to be the lead either." It was bad enough being on stage, but at least I was in the back. It would be horrible being up front like Veronique. And it wasn't like I sang all that well anyway. "Why can't we just leave everything the way it is?" I asked.

"I agree," Aaliyah added. "I don't want to be the lead. India doesn't want to be the lead. Let's just keep winning with what we've got."

Diamond kept pushing. "We could still win with one of us singing the lead. There are four levels of this contest and four of us—"

"How many ways do I have to tell you no?" Aaliyah asked, sounding like one of our parents. She crossed her arms.

"Okay, then. Let's do songs that don't have leads."

Aaliyah shrugged. "Ain't nothin' but a thang to me. But on the real, I think we should just leave everything the way it is. And if anyone asks me, that's what I'm sayin'."

Diamond turned to me, looking like she wanted me on her side.

I shrugged. "I agree with Aaliyah," I said softly.

"Whatever, whatever." Diamond stomped over to the other side of the room, far away from us.

Aaliyah had tried to shut Diamond down, but I knew this

wasn't going to be the end. Not with Diamond. She'd been my best friend forever, and I knew her well.

I also knew what this was all about. It was about school and how now the guys were paying more attention to Veronique than they were paying to her. Diamond didn't like that; she wasn't having it.

She wanted the attention. She wanted the lead. And if there was one thing I knew, it was that what Diamond wanted, Diamond got.

I sighed as I looked at my best friend, still pouting in the corner.

Nope, this wasn't over. Not now. Not yet.

chapter 7

I knew this was going to be a rough ride.

It was almost Christmas. My mom and dad's favorite time of the year. They dragged me to so many holiday parties it wasn't even funny. Just thinking about all of that food made me want to run to the golden arches right away and get an apple pie.

But I had made up my mind. I was going to be strong. Between now and February, for the next fifty-eight days, I wasn't going to eat a thing.

Okay, so, maybe I would have to eat a little. But that's all it would be. Just a little. And only when I got really, really hungry. If I could do that, then by the time we got to San Francisco for the state finals, I would be looking good.

I had come up with this plan last night and was so excited. This was the first time I'd ever come up with something that I was sure would work.

But this morning, I saw just how hard this was going to be—especially when there was food, or talk of food, all around you.

It started first with Tova. I thought my mother would be easy—if I said I wasn't hungry, she wouldn't mind. She thought I ate too much anyway. So when I said that for breakfast I only wanted a banana—which I didn't eat—she was fine. But then she was the first one to make it hard for me.

"Jill called," she said, referring to my cousin. "She wants you to help her sell some chocolate candy for a fund-raiser she's participating in at her school."

Chocolate candy! Why did my mother have to bring that up? By the time I left my house, I was already starving.

Then I got to first period—French class. I wanted to just die when Ms. Cecily said, "Today we're going to practice ordering food in a restaurant. Pair off."

I couldn't believe it. I had to sit there with Riley and pretend that we were in a café. I didn't care how bad I mispronounced those words. I still knew that *pâtés* was pasta and *pommes frites* were French fries and *gâteau* was cake. And what was way worse was that my all-time favorite food—hamburger—was the same in English *and* French. So I couldn't even pretend that I was talking about something else.

Then, in geometry, I don't know why, but every triangle Mr. Berg drew on the board looked like a slice of lemon meringue pie. And every rectangle looked like a Snickers bar.

By the time the bell rang for lunch, my stomach was rumbling because I hadn't had one bite of food. And I had a headache because of all that food that was dancing around in my head.

"So, what's up?" Aaliyah asked after I sat down at the table next to her and made no move to go to the food line. "You're not going to buy lunch?"

"No." And then my stomach growled. Loud. Like it was really mad at me. I took a quick peek at her plate and had to sit on my hands so I wouldn't snatch her hamburger. And then my stomach made some more noise. This time, it was so loud, I was embarrassed. "I'm not very hungry," I said, even though my stomach was trying to tell everybody that I was lying.

"You've gotta eat something," Diamond said before she stuffed her mouth with her grilled cheese sandwich. "We've got to keep up our energy. It takes a lot of stamina to be a true diva, you know."

"I had a big breakfast." I hoped that lie would get my best friends to stop talking about food. All of this talk and all of these smells had me feeling like I was on the edge.

"I had a big breakfast, too," Veronique piped in. "But this pizza is off the chain." She sucked a long string of cheese between her lips. "You sure you don't want a piece?"

What I wanted was to stand up and scream. They were supposed to be my best friends, but today, they were more like my big-time enemies. Throwing all of this food in my face. How was I supposed to lose weight with all of this?

"Dang!" Diamond looked at her watch, then stuffed the rest of her sandwich in her mouth. "I gotta get out of here. I'm still doing makeup work to get my grades up before finals."

Veronique stood up, too. "Wait up. I'll go with you. I have to stop by my locker before next period."

I eyed the pizza crust that Veronique, left on her plate and hoped that she would leave her tray right there. Then I would sneak a bite—just a little one. But she took her plate away, leaving me with nothing.

"Let's meet up after school," Diamond said.

Aaliyah and I nodded.

"Holla!"

I waved, but as soon as I turned back to the table, Aaliyah jumped on me. "So, what's the real deal?" She frowned like she knew something was up. I guess that's why she was my bestest—she knew me really well. But even though we were close, I wasn't sure if I wanted to tell Aaliyah. I didn't want anyone making fun of me. But if anyone could help, it would be Aaliyah.

"Well, it's not like something's really up. I'm just trying to lose some weight." And then my stomach rumbled again.

"Why?" she said, as if that was the most ridiculous thing she'd ever heard.

"Because in case you haven't noticed, I'm fat."

"No, you're not. You're healthy."

"That's just another word for fat. I've heard them all—big-boned, solid, healthy—it all just means fat."

"That's ridiculous, India."

"Spoken like a girl who wears a size four."

"It doesn't matter what size you wear. We're Black. And everyone knows that Black women carry more, especially in our hips and legs."

That cracked me up. "Black women carry more? What are you carrying?"

Aaliyah pressed her lips together and started rocking her head, making her long braids sway from side to side. "I may be small-boned, but I'm still carrying a little junk in my trunk." She snapped her fingers three times.

"You don't even have a trunk!" I laughed and my bestest laughed with me. But then I said, "Seriously, I just want to lose a little weight."

Aaliyah nodded slowly, as if now she understood. "I guess that's okay. And it can't hurt. . . ."

I smiled.

She held up her finger. "If . . . you're doing this for yourself. . . ."

I nodded. "I am—"

She interrupted me. "And . . . you do it healthily. You can't just not eat."

Now I knew how Diamond felt. Aaliyah was always the sensible one—sometimes she was too sensible when all you wanted was a friend.

She said, "Why don't you go to Weight Watchers or something?"

Ewww. I could not believe she said that. Weight Watchers? Did she really want me to walk into one of those meetings with all of those fat ladies? How was that supposed to help me? And what if someone I knew found out? Everyone would laugh at me for sure!

"I know what you're thinking," Aaliyah said. "But you don't have to go to a Weight Watchers meeting. You can do it all online."

"No way!" I shook my head.

"I can come over to your house," she began as if she hadn't heard me say no, "and we can look it up online together. Weight Watchers would be the rational way to do this."

Oh, brother! I wasn't even thinking about being rational. I just wanted this weight off—and fast.

"I'll think about it," I said, just to shut her up. "But since I just want to lose a little, I might be able to do it by myself. Just promise me you won't say anything to Diamond or Vee."

She frowned. "Why not?"

"I don't want them to make fun of me."

"They wouldn't do that." Aaliyah scrunched her face. "The only thing Diamond or Vee would say is that you're fine just the way you are. And I would agree with them."

I wanted to tell my bestest that was easy for her to say, since she was almost as tall as I was. But at five feet eight inches, she was less than half my size. I didn't say anything else, though, as she stood up and took her tray away. When she came back, she grabbed her backpack, and we walked out of the cafeteria together.

"Catch ya later."

I nodded as my stomach growled again. But this time, a little bit of ache came with it. And my head hurt more, too. But I kept focused. And I kept thinking—all I had to do was make it through today. And then, I would only have fifty-seven more days to go.

"What's wrong, honey?" Tova pressed the back of her hand on my forehead like she always did. "You don't look so good."

I shook my head. "I don't feel well," I told her, just like I'd told my friends a little while ago at school. I really was sick. My stomach hurt. My head hurt. And I felt dizzy.

"Go up to bed and I'll make you some soup."

Soup. I never really liked soup, because it didn't fill me up. But right about now, I could imagine eating a big ole pot. I wasn't going to do that, though. I'd made it all the way through school without eating anything. All I had to do was hang in there for a few more hours and I would have made it through the whole day. I wasn't going to punk out now.

"I'm too sick, Tova." I held my stomach.

"Oh, honey. Go on to your room and I'll check on you in a little while."

It seemed to take two days to get to my bedroom, but as soon as I got in there, I fell right onto my bed. Just being able to lie down helped my head a little bit. But it didn't do a thing for my stomach. It was growling and twirling and rumbling, like it was never going to stop.

I looked at my closet and thought about the box in there. No, I wasn't about to mess up like that. Just a few more hours. I just had to make it through this first day.

But my bedroom was too quiet. All I could think about were the donuts in my closet and how my stomach was totally empty. *One donut wouldn't hurt,* I thought. And then I remembered reading one time that eating actually helped your metabolism and made you burn calories. Maybe if I had a donut, it would be even better than not eating anything all day.

"Just one donut," I promised myself as I pulled down my stash.

It felt like heaven—that first bite. I had never tasted a donut so, so good. Then I decided that two was probably better than one.

I didn't have any control after that. One donut after another. And then, the cakes. I didn't stop until I was looking down at the bottom of the empty shoe box.

I couldn't believe it. After working so hard all day. Now I was really sick, and not just in my stomach. Deep inside I felt way, way worse—like I was a big ole failure. I couldn't do a doggone thing right.

I lay back on my bed, and even though I wanted to cry, I didn't. I just had to come up with another plan.

First, I wouldn't buy any more snacks. I wouldn't keep a stash in my room. Then, I would find a different way not to eat again—at least not for the next fifty-seven days.

chapter 8

It must be so cool to be you right about now."

Okay, now see—I knew I had a lot of problems, but I didn't know that one of them was my hearing. I stared at my cousin Jill through the mirror and waited for her to add the punch line to that joke. But she just sat on my bed, shuffling through my jewelry box.

So I asked her, "What did you say?" because I just knew that I'd heard her wrong.

"It must be so cool to be you," she repeated, sounding like she really meant it. "You have all these cool friends. And now you're in this cool group. And you're making all of this cool stuff." She held up one of my necklaces that was kind of heavy with all the charms I'd added to it. The way she sighed, you would have thought Jill had never seen anything so beautiful. "Your life is the best right about now."

I don't think I ever imagined anyone saying that about my life, especially not Jill. To me, my sixteen-year-old cousin was the cool one. With her long legs, blond hair that came to her

46

waist, and Angelina Jolie lips, I expected to hear the news any day that she was dropping out of Beverly Hills High to become a model—just like our mothers.

"I think I want this one," Jill said, holding up one of the double-strand chain belts I'd made.

I'd told her that she could choose any one of my pieces and it would be her Christmas gift.

"No, I want this." Now she was holding up the necklace with the charms. "I don't know. I can't decide." Then she grinned at me. "Can I have both? One for Christmas and one for my birthday?"

I frowned. "Your birthday's not until May."

"Please!" she begged and hooked the necklace around her neck. "If you give me both now, you won't have to give me anything in May."

What I wanted to tell her was that I didn't plan to give her anything in May anyway. I never gave her a birthday gift—never even gave her a Christmas gift. Jill was only getting something now because she and her mother had come over for dinner.

Jill was my favorite cousin on my mother's side (really, she was my only cousin on my mother's side), but we didn't spend that much time together. Jill and her parents, my aunt Emelie and uncle Alf, lived right in Los Angeles—in the Hollywood Hills. And although that wasn't far from where we lived in Ladera Heights, I didn't get to see her all that often. I wasn't sure why, but I think it had something to do with my uncle not really liking us. Whenever Aunt Emelie and Jill came to visit, Uncle Alf never came with them—unless it was a holiday. And then he always looked like he was ready to leave.

One time, when I was standing in my secret place listening to my parents talk, I heard my dad say that Uncle Alf didn't like his "Negro" side of the family. Although my dad had laughed, that had made me feel bad. I hated when Black people talked about white people around me. And I hated it the other way around, too. I never knew what to do, since I was both—Black and white. It was just another one of those things that made my whole life miserable.

"So," Jill continued, now hooking the chain belt around her waist as if I'd already told her that she could have both, "did you ever think that the Divine Divas were going to be like totally this big?"

I sat on the bed and shook my head. "Nope. And it's kinda scary sometimes."

"Yeah, I can see how it can be scary, being on that humongous stage. But it's got to be way cool, too. When I watched you at the Kodak Theatre, I was wishing that I was you!"

I frowned and wondered if Jill had really taken a good look at these jeans I was wearing. I'd almost cried last week when Tova had insisted that I needed to get some new jeans because all the ones I had were too tight. Now, not only was I almost two hundred pounds, but I was a size eighteen, too!

"How was it? Being on that stage?"

I shrugged. "It was okay."

Jill frowned. "Just okay?"

"Well, you know . . ." And then I stopped. I wasn't sure how much I wanted to tell Jill. Sure, she was my cousin, but I wasn't as close to her as I was to Aaliyah. Or even Diamond and Veronique.

"You don't like singing?" she asked.

"That's not it."

"You don't like dancing?"

"I'm not crazy about that part."

"Why not?" Jill stood up, busted a move, swung her hands up in the air, and sang the words from Timbaland's song, *"Baby, if you strip, you can get a tip. 'Cause I like you just the way you are!"* She giggled. "Shoot," she said, finally sitting down, "nobody better ask me to get on the stage and dance. I'll be all over it."

I couldn't imagine *anyone* asking Jill to dance. I hated to say it, but my cousin moved just like a white girl.

"So, what's your problem, Indy?"

"I don't know. I guess . . . you know, I don't look as good up there as my friends."

She looked at me for a moment, and then it was like she got it. "Oh, because you're fat."

My eyes opened wider than they ever had before. Yeah, I was fat, but I didn't need her to say that. None of my BFFs would have ever said that out loud.

"Why are you staring at me?" Jill asked.

It wasn't until she said it that I realized I was growling at her. But she had hurt all of my feelings for real.

Jill said, "I was just sayin', you're a little bit on the fat side."

"Okay, can you stop saying that?"

She shrugged. "I didn't mean anything by it."

I didn't say another word. All I did was wish that my mother or her mother would come up to my room right now and tell Jill it was time for them to go—even though we hadn't even eaten dinner yet. Didn't matter. I wanted Jill out . . . of . . . here!

"So what? You're not speaking to me now?"

I rolled my eyes and didn't part my lips. It took everything in me not to rip my necklace off her skinny neck. But the necklace was way too pretty to mess up.

"Well," Jill bounced on the bed and looked straight at me like she didn't care if I was mad. "If you're not talking to me, I guess that means you're not listening either."

She was right about that. I mean, it was hard not to listen, since she was sitting right in front of my face. But I wasn't going to have a conversation with her. I wasn't going to talk to anyone who would walk right into my house and call me fat.

"Then I guess you don't want to hear the secret I have. The secret that stops you from being fat."

Okay, now see—she wasn't playing fair. How was I supposed to ignore her now? I didn't even want to look up, but I couldn't help it. If Jill had a secret that would stop me from being fat, I needed to hear it.

I looked up, and my cousin smiled. And I frowned. Now I wondered if she really had something, or was that just a trick to get me to speak to her? "What kind of secret?" I asked. I hoped that I still sounded like I was mad, because I was. But I could get over it for a little while. I needed to know something, because nothing I was doing was working.

Not eating all day on Wednesday had been a disaster. Thursday and yesterday had been a little bit better—I hadn't eaten any French fries at all. And since I was trying not to have a stash box anymore, I'd only eaten three apple pies that I'd gotten from the golden arches. But I was going to have to do a whole lot more than that if I wanted to lose some real weight.

Jill scooted closer to me on the bed. "I know a way where you can eat all you want and never get fat," she whispered. "Lots of girls in my school do it."

"Do what?" All of my mad was gone now.

"I'll tell you under one condition." And she held up the belt I'd made. "Can I have the necklace *and* this?"

If it was going to help me, she could have every single piece of jewelry I'd ever made.

She glanced toward my bedroom door even though it was closed. But she still kept her voice low. "All you have to do is throw up after you eat."

I leaned away from Jill and scrunched up my face. "Ewww. That's disgusting." I thought about the few times when I'd been sick and had thrown up. That was way nasty. Throwing up always made me sicker! Why would anyone want to throw up if they didn't have to?

She shrugged. "You said you didn't want to be fat anymore. And this works. You can't be fat if you don't keep the food inside of you."

Okay, so, I didn't want to be fat. But did I want to be nasty?

Jill must have read my mind, because she said, "Look, everybody's doing it."

I didn't know anyone doing that. "Are you?"

She shrugged a little. "Sometimes." And then she looked at me. "Okay, I do it every day. After dinner."

My mouth was all the way open. "Why would *you* do that?" I just couldn't imagine my cousin even thinking about being fat. She wore a size two.

"Because sometimes I *feel* fat. So this just helps to make sure that I never *get* fat."

"I can't believe that you have to throw up anything."

"Well, it works. I learned about it from some of the girls in my school. And you read about it all the time—all the actresses in Hollywood are doing it. And I bet if you asked your mom or my mom, they did it. I think all the models do it."

I couldn't imagine my mom doing anything like this. I know she said that in her modeling days she did whatever she had to do to stay skinny. But I would bet all of my allowance that Tova never threw up. It was way too disgusting for her.

It must have been the way I was shaking my head that made Jill add, "Indy, there's nothing wrong with it. Some people call it an eating disorder, but there's nothing disorderly about it if it works."

Now, I had heard of eating disorders. Reporters on all of those Entertainment programs talked about it all the time. And like Jill said, the reporters were always talking about some actress or model. And then that interviewer Nicolette had asked Tova if she'd ever had any eating disorders.

But now that Jill was actually *describing* what an eating disorder was, it just didn't seem like anything I could do. But still I asked, "So what do you do . . . exactly?"

Without saying a word, Jill stood up, and I followed her to my computer. As she typed, she talked. "This is what I did the first time. I went to this site. Here you go." She swiveled the computer screen toward me.

I read the top of the page. It said something about pro-bulimia.

"You don't have to read all of this now, but this will tell you how to throw up. All you have to do is put your fingers down your throat." Because I didn't say a word, Jill added, "It can't be bad if it's on the 'Net."

We were staring at that page so hard that when we heard the knock on my door, it made us jump out of our chairs.

"Hey," my dad said when he opened the door and came inside. "I'm looking for my favorite daughter."

"I'm here, Daddy," I said, rushing over and hugging him. There was no way I wanted him to see what we were looking at on the computer. "I'm your favorite . . . and *only* daughter."

"Oh, that's right." He laughed. "And I'm looking for my favorite niece."

Jill jumped up and hugged my father, too. "Uncle Marvin, I'm your *only* niece."

"But you're still my favorite." My father looked over the top of my head at my computer. "What're you guys doing up here?"

My heart was beating way hard. I didn't want my dad to know anything about what Jill had been telling me.

"Nothing, Uncle Marvin." Jill sat on my bed all nonchalant. "I was just showing India some stuff from my school."

I glanced at my computer, and the screen was black. Jill had turned it off. She was sixteen; I guess she really knew how to do all that sneaky stuff.

"I bet y'all are talking about boys." My father laughed.

Jill laughed with my dad, but I didn't find anything funny. Why would I be talking about boys when no boys—except for Riley—even talked to me.

"No, Uncle Marvin. Not boys. Just girl stuff."

"Uh-huh." My dad made that sound like he didn't believe us. "Well, y'all get ready to come on downstairs for dinner." He looked at me. "You know your mother. Be on time."

"Yes, Daddy."

Jill waited until my dad closed the door before she said, "Later on, just go back online and check out the instructions. It's not hard." She paused a second. "You will have to cut down a little on your eating to make this really work. And if you drink a lot of water, it will help the food to float in your stomach," she explained like an expert. "That will make it so much easier to throw up."

All I could say was, "We'd better get down to dinner."

There was just no way I could do it. Putting my fingers down my throat? Ugh! It was too horrible to even think about.

"Okay, who wants cake!" my dad said, bringing in the big ole square cake with thick green and white icing.

"I couldn't eat another thing," my aunt Emelie said.

"I don't want any either," my mother said, too.

I never understood that about my mom. She'd cook all of this food and bake all of this dessert and then never eat it. And she didn't want me to eat it either. I guess it was just supposed to all be for my dad.

Jill said, "I wanna piece" and licked her lips.

Of course she did. And I wanted a piece, too. A big piece. But being skinny in San Francisco was still on my mind.

"I don't want a piece." I shook my head as if I really meant that and kept my eyes off that cake. Because if I looked at it anymore, it would be so over.

"Honey, that's very good." The way my mother was smiling at me, you would have thought I'd just brought home all As on my report card.

"What did you do, India?" my aunt Emelie asked, clueless to what my mom was complimenting me about.

I opened my mouth but didn't get a chance to say anything before my mother explained to her sister how her fat daughter was trying not to eat so much. She didn't exactly use the word *fat,* but everyone at the table knew what she meant.

And then my aunt did what my mom was doing. She smiled at me. Like not eating a piece of cake was something so special.

"You should have at least one little piece," Jill said.

My mom and Aunt Emelie turned to Jill. And both of their smiles were gone.

"Jill, don't tempt her," my mother said. "We all have to be supportive of India."

My cousin shrugged. "Indy and I've already talked." She continued the conversation as if I was invisible. "I'm probably the most supportive one here."

I watched as Jill slipped another forkful of cake into her mouth. And this time, I was the one who licked my lips.

I couldn't do it. I couldn't just sit here and watch Jill eat this cake and not have any myself. I wouldn't be able to sleep all night, knowing that the cake was in the kitchen if I didn't have a little piece.

But if I had a piece of cake, that would be bad—unless I did what Jill said and got rid of it.

Looking across the table, I smiled at my cousin. And when Jill smiled back, I could tell that she knew what I was thinking. I was going to take her advice. I was going to be skinny.

It had taken hours to get this piece of cake.

I had to wait until Jill and Aunt Emelie left. And then I had to wait until my parents went into their bedroom. At least they weren't staying up late tonight. I thought that since it was Saturday, they'd be in the family room watching TV. But they were getting all lovey-dovey, which was all right with me.

When they'd been in their bedroom for fifteen minutes, I tiptoed into the kitchen.

I cut a big piece of cake because I didn't want to have to sneak back for a second one. And now I was just eating it slowly. This cake was so good, but I wasn't that focused on what I was eating. All of my attention was on my computer.

I read the postings on bulimia so much that I felt like I was studying for a test. But no matter how many times I looked over it, it still seemed pretty disgusting to me.

Slowly, I licked the green icing off all my fingers, then turned off my computer. I had to do this, and I had to do this now. Especially since I'd just finished that jumbo slice of cake.

Inside the bathroom, I stared at the toilet for only a little while before I got on my knees, took a deep breath, and then stuck my fingers down my throat.

I gagged. Over and over. I couldn't stop gagging. Even though nothing came out, it still felt disgusting.

I leaned back for a little while. Thought about the cake. Thought even more about being on stage in San Francisco. I just had to do this.

This time, I lowered my head deeper into the toilet, took

another breath, and pushed my fingers as far back as I could. I didn't stop until it came up. All of it. Everything I'd just eaten.

"Ewww." I jumped up and stuck my hand under the faucet, making the water as hot as I could. "Disgusting!" I kept saying over and over again.

I didn't move away from that water until my fingers began to look like they belonged to a wrinkled old lady. Then I flushed the toilet and stumbled all the way to my bed before I fell on it.

I was totally out of breath as I stared at my ceiling.

That was so bad. No, it was way worse than bad. It was completely, totally disgusting.

But it had worked.

And now I would just wait and see if this worked all the way for real.

chapter 9

Diamond flipped her hair over her shoulder like she'd been doing all day. For her birthday, she'd had her hair streaked with a mahogany tint, and I guessed she wanted to make sure that we all noticed—as if there had been a way to miss it, since she also told us about it at least fifty times since we'd met up for lunch.

"Okay," Diamond shouted, "I want to give a toast." I laughed with my other BFFs as Diamond jumped up from her chair and raised her glass. Sometimes, my girl was so dramatic. Just like my mother. I swear, I wondered if we'd been switched at birth, because Diamond acted way more like my mother than I did.

"Diamond," Aaliyah began, "it's your birthday. You cannot give your own toast," she said like she knew all the toasting rules.

"But not one of you," she pointed her fingers in our faces, "stood up to give me my rightful toast. So I'm doing it myself."

She held her strawberry shake high in the air, then waited until we did the same. I lifted my glass of water.

"Okay, to the best friends in the whole wide world," Diamond said. "Thank you for sharing this most special birthday with me. As you already know, I was fine at fifteen, but I'll be bringing sexy back at sixteen." She did that hair-whipping-shoulder-thing again.

Veronique, Aaliyah, and I groaned together, "Oh, brother!" even though we were still grinning.

But that didn't stop Diamond's roll. "And I also want to thank you all for this fabulous gift." She stopped and held up the almost-one-hundred-dollar pen that the three of us had chipped in and bought for her. Veronique had gone crazy when she'd found out how much the pen had cost. But she hadn't complained for long—I guess she remembered how we all bought her an MP3 player for *her* birthday.

"Y'all know I'm gonna be signing lots of autographs with this," Diamond continued. "So thank you for finally recognizing me for the VIP that I was born to be and the star that I already am."

Again we all groaned, but in the next second we were cracking up. You just had to love Diamond. I just wished that I had half her cool.

"And," Diamond went on, "thank you for being Divine Divas with me. We're gonna blow up the spot in San Fran, we're gonna rock them in the NYC, and then we're gonna step out and wrap it up in Miami. We're gonna win it all!"

We cheered and clicked our glasses together. Normally I would have been way embarrassed to be making so much noise in the restaurant, but even the people who were sitting around us clapped, like they knew who we were. And that made me feel kinda special.

We took a sip from our glasses, then the waiters came

out, carrying a cake with a couple of candles flickering in the middle.

"Happy birthday to you. . . ."

As they sang, Diamond pushed her hand against her chest like she was so surprised. Please! Since we were thirteen, we came to the Ivy for her birthday every year. And every year, we brought a cake. And every year, the waiters came out and sang. And every year, she made that surprise face.

Straight drama!

If this singing thing didn't work out, Diamond definitely needed to keep the pen we'd given her. 'Cause she had a big future as an actress in somebody's movie. She was right—she was gonna be signing lots of autographs.

"Okay, let me cut it." Diamond held up the knife, and in as dramatic a motion as she could make, she slipped the knife down the center of the cake.

My mouth was already watering as I stared at the two-layer chocolate cake that was dripping in thick icing. But I'd made a promise—I wasn't going to have a piece. After throwing up last night, I had done my best not to eat too much today. Even now, as my friends all had hamburgers, I'd only had a salad. I didn't even know how I made it through lunch. I guess thinking about San Francisco was really helping.

But this cake was looking too good. I turned my chair a little so it wouldn't be right in front of my face.

"Of course, I get the first piece because it's my birthday and now I'm older than all y'all." She sliced a second piece. "And now, here's one for you, India."

I shook my head. "No, thank you."

Diamond froze with the knife still raised in the air, like she was about to cut somebody. "What do you mean you're not going to have a piece of *my* cake?"

"I don't want a piece. I'm not very hungry."

"This is not about being hungry. No one's ever hungry for dessert. Plus, it's my birthday. You *have* to have a piece."

It would have been easier to just take the cake, but I didn't want to mess up. "Give it to Aaliyah," I said, taking the plate from Diamond and pushing it as fast as I could in front of my bestest.

Diamond was still frozen and frowning. "Are you on a diet or something?"

"No!" I said and glanced at Aaliyah. But I didn't have to worry. My bestest wouldn't give me up.

"Then you have to have a piece of my cake!" she whined.

How had this become all about Diamond? I didn't want the cake, but I took the slice because she would've pressed me for the next five hours if I hadn't.

I was mad at first. Then I took a little bite and I was back in heaven again.

It was kinda quiet as we all sat there eating. I kept eating—and kept drinking my water.

Diamond was the first to talk. "We've got to start thinking about what we're gonna wear in San Fran," she announced in a tone that said finding outfits for a contest that was still two months away was way urgent.

"We got plenty of time, my sistah." Veronique waved Diamond's words away. "Plus, I wanna get a few more paychecks from Pastor so that I'll really have something to shop with."

"We can never start shopping too early," Diamond said. "So that we can take our time. Unless," she said as she turned to me, "Drama Mama is going to work with her designers again."

I shrugged. Even though I felt good about my plan to be skinny, I wasn't ready to go shopping or talk about clothes. "I haven't asked Tova."

"We should all go together and ask Drama Mama. We can

60

do it when we get back to rehearsals after New Year's. If we do it together, your mother will never be able to tell us no."

"I can't believe we're not rehearsing this week," Aaliyah piped in. "I thought Sybil would've had us working every day while we were on Christmas break."

"I guess she knows a good thing when she sees it," Veronique said as she sliced herself another small piece of cake.

Sometimes I hated watching Veronique eat. She ate as much as I did, but she never gained a single pound. I guess it was a good thing, because she was the shortest of us—at least four inches shorter than me. If she gained any weight, she would've been way fatter than me.

Veronique said, "Sybil knows we're stars already."

I was kinda surprised to hear Veronique saying that. It was usually Diamond who was kinda conceited with all that stuff about being a star. But since we'd won the L.A. competition, Veronique was beginning to sound more and more like Diamond.

And then Veronique made a big mistake and said, "Speaking of rehearsals, I have some ideas about the Divine Divas that I wanted to talk to Sybil and you guys about."

Diamond frowned. "What kind of ideas?"

Uh-oh, I thought and slipped the last little piece of cake on my plate into my mouth.

"I haven't thought it all the way through," Veronique said, "but I was thinking that I needed to do a little more as the lead. I need to figure out ways to really get the crowd involved."

When Diamond raised her eyebrows, I took a big ole gulp of water. This looked like it could turn into a BFF fight; I would need a lot more cake to help me handle it. As Veronique broke down what she was talking about to Diamond, I cut another piece—a little bigger this time.

"But I don't have it all worked out in my head yet," Veronique continued. "I'll be ready when we get back to rehearsals."

"Any suggestions you have need to be run by me first," Diamond demanded, like she owned the Divine Divas or something.

"I just said," Veronique began, her voice now filled with as much attitude as Diamond's, "I was going to run it by *you all* and Sybil."

"And I just said that you need to tell us first. This isn't Sybil's group, it's ours. And we need to make decisions together." Diamond squinted. "Together and equally."

"My peeps," Aaliyah said before Veronique could respond. "This is supposed to be a birthday slash Christmas celebration. We're not the Divine Divas right now, so can we not talk about this?"

"Oh, see, that's where you got it wrong." Diamond wiggled her neck. "We're always Divine Divas . . . at least I am."

Aaliyah shrugged. "I'm just sayin', we're supposed to be just peeps hanging right now. Not singers."

I didn't say a thing. Just cut myself a third piece of cake.

With her voice back to normal, Veronique said, "Diamond, you don't have anything to worry about. We're a group. I wouldn't do anything without talking to all of you."

But Diamond was not about to let it go. "Just so you know."

"What do you mean by that?" Veronique frowned.

"Can we change the subject?" Aaliyah pleaded. "I don't feel like getting into a fight the day before Christmas."

"Who said anything about fighting," Diamond asked, although she sounded like she was ready for a big ole knockdown, drag out.

Aaliyah said, "With the way you and Vee are going at it. I mean, where's your holiday spirit?"

"I just lost mine." Diamond stood, shoved her bag onto her shoulder, then grabbed her gift. "Thanks a lot," she said, although I didn't hear any kind of gratitude in her voice. "For everything." And then she stomped away like the spoiled brat that everyone said she was. We were all supposed to be riding with Aaliyah's dad. But I guess Diamond was going to find her own way home.

I took the last bite of my third piece of cake, then turned to Veronique and Aaliyah.

"What just happened?" Veronique asked, sounding confused.

Aaliyah shrugged. "I don't know. She's mad about something."

I said, "I can't believe she didn't even take the rest of this cake with her."

Veronique ignored what I said. Her eyes were squinted like she was thinking heavy and trying to figure it out. "Have you guys noticed anything different about Diamond?"

At first, Aaliyah and I didn't say a word.

Veronique said, "Every time we talk about the Divine Divas, she seems kinda stressed."

"I don't know what's wrong with her," Aaliyah said.

I just shrugged my shoulders and scraped the crumbs off my plate. If Aaliyah wasn't going to say anything about Diamond's real problem, then I wasn't about to give Diamond up either. It didn't matter if Aaliyah and I said anything right now anyway. It was all going to come out soon because there was no way Diamond was going to just walk away. She didn't live like that.

And when it came out, it was going to be ugly. Because the thing was, Diamond didn't play. But here's the other thing—neither did Veronique.

"Well, as our girl would say, whatever, whatever. Y'all ready to roll?" Veronique stood.

Aaliyah pulled her cell from her purse. "Let me call my dad. He said he'd be just ten minutes away."

"Uh, you guys go on without me. My mom's coming." I hugged Aaliyah. "Have a merry Christmas."

"You're not gonna walk out with us?" Aaliyah asked.

"No." I had a hard time looking at my bestest when I added, "I have to go to the bathroom."

"Okay. I'll call you tomorrow, my sistah," Veronique said before she hugged me.

I watched the two of them walk out together before I drank almost half a glass of water, then went right into the bathroom. I didn't want to take the chance and wait until I got home. I wanted to get rid of all the cake—and the salad—I'd eaten right now.

I was starting to get it. Five minutes later, I was on my way home. On my way home—empty and happy.

I peeked around the corner; my mother and father were just resting on the couch, watching some kind of news program. How boring was that for Christmas Eve, but it worked for me right now. I tiptoed into their bedroom.

Inside their bathroom, I pulled the scale out from under my mother's sink and stared at it. I always hated these things, but I had to know.

Softly, I put one foot on, then the other. I didn't look down—not right away. But when I did, I felt my eyes open way wide.

The last time I'd gone to the doctor, I'd weighed almost 200 pounds. But now the scale said 195.

I got off and stepped back on again. Yup, one hundred ninety-five. Could I have lost almost five pounds in just two days?

I slipped the scale back under the sink, then ran as softly as I could down the hall to my bedroom. This was way exciting.

I had to call Jill and tell her. And give her a big-time thank you. But first I grabbed my jewelry box. For what my cousin had done for me, I needed to give her something special. I held up the belt that she'd wanted so badly, and then I reached for my phone.

chapter 10

Even though it had only been a week and two days, it felt like I hadn't seen my BFFs since forever.

That's why we'd decided on our first day back to school after the Christmas holiday to meet up early. But as crowded as the halls were, it seemed like everyone had the same idea.

"Girl, you are rocking those shoes," Veronique said as Diamond strutted back and forth in her navy platform pumps.

"Aren't they fierce? My first pair of real designer shoes. You know I almost died when I opened the box and saw Gucci on the label."

"I know that's right," Veronique said. "I'll be forty before I have a Gucci anything."

"And check these out." We all said "aahh" when Diamond showed us her Chanel sunglasses. "You know I was hopin' for a car as a double birthday-Christmas gift, but the judge said they needed to see more responsibility from me."

"And you're okay with that?" Veronique asked.

Diamond shrugged. "What can I do? It's not like I have any

money for a car. I'll just have to show them how responsible I really am. Give me a couple of weeks—I'll get my ride."

I was way, way shocked that Diamond wasn't upset. But knowing my best friend, she was already working it out, and I believed her when she said she'd have that car soon.

Diamond said, "Even without the car, my dad and the judge really did it up for my sixteenth. Do you know how much these cost?"

We were standing in the hallway, but Diamond slapped those glasses on like the sun was shining through the roof!

We all laughed, and then Veronique turned to Aaliyah. "And what are you up to, my sistah? You look pretty good yourself."

"Yeah," I added and grinned at my bestest. I'd never seen Aaliyah in a hat before, but she was sporting this beret, kinda twisted to the side, like she was a French girl or something.

"Yeah, you look really cute." Diamond laughed. "Looking like Picasso."

Aaliyah tried to frown, even though she was really grinning. "What you know about Picasso?"

"Honey, you're not the only one who knows a little somethin' somethin' 'bout art."

We laughed again. I had to admit, my best friends did look good. Even Veronique was rollin' in something new—camouflage capris that tied at the bottom. I was the only one who hadn't worn something from my Christmas gifts. But I had a good reason. Everything I'd gotten for Christmas was already getting kinda big on me. That was the best gift of all—in ten days, I'd lost a little more than ten more pounds.

It was major—learning how to get rid of the calories before they went to live on my legs and thighs and stomach. It was way cool. And it didn't seem so nasty anymore.

"You look good, too, India," Diamond said. She stepped back and looked me up and down as if she was giving me a special examination. "Something's different about you, too." She stopped. Scanned my peasant skirt and T-shirt, trying to figure it out. "What did you do? Cut your hair?"

"Nope." I shook my head, even though I did have it pulled back in a loose ponytail.

"But there's something . . . ," Diamond said like she was some kind of detective and she was going to figure it out.

"Nothing's different about me." And that was the truth, if you didn't count the ten pounds I'd lost, or my hair being pulled back, or the little bit of blush I wore that didn't make my skin look so pink.

But can I tell you—I was feeling all the way good because Diamond had noticed something.

"Well, I think we all look awesome," Veronique said, and we gave each other high fives.

"We're supposed to," Diamond added. "We're the Divine Divas."

"Hey, Veronique!" It sounded like a chorus of voices that called out her name.

I turned just in time to see a group of boys from the basketball team strolling by in their varsity jackets. And they were all grinning at us. Well, maybe not us. All of their smiles were for Veronique.

"Hey." She waved back to them, all the time grinning.

Veronique was sure soaking up the glory way more than even Diamond. So, I was not hardly surprised when Diamond leaned against her locker, with her arms all crossed and stared Veronique down as she waved and giggled at all the boys.

Then the worst thing in the world happened—Jason Xavier walked by. And he called out to Veronique, too. "What's up, Vee?"

Okay, now see—this was way worse than straight drama. This was straight trouble. I didn't even want to look at Diamond, 'cause I knew she had to be getting ready to beat somebody down. Jason was her man—or at least he used to be. According to Diamond, she and Jason—or Jax, as everyone called him—were way serious (like in love) at the beginning of the semester. They'd been feeling each other so much that one night, Jax took Diamond to a hotel so that they could spend the night together.

But something happened—they didn't stay out all night, and then they even stopped seeing each other—really fast. Just a couple of days after that, Jax was hanging with his old girlfriend—Jayde Monroe.

Diamond never talked about Jax anymore, but the way she was staring him down right now, I was getting scared myself. I just hoped she didn't do anything like try to curse him out or smack him, 'cause Holy Cross Prep didn't play any of that. You would get a three-day suspension for using foul language and a week suspension for violence—no questions asked, no explanations needed.

With the way Diamond slammed her locker shut, I knew all the good feelings of glad-to-be-back-with-my-best-friends were gone.

Diamond said, "When we start rehearsals this week, there's something I want to talk about."

She was glaring at me and Aaliyah, but I knew what she said was meant for Veronique. I just wasn't sure Veronique had heard her. She was still grinning and waving like she was some big-time star.

Diamond said, "We need to talk about who's going to do the lead in San Fran."

Veronique swiveled around. "What?"

I guess she *had* heard Diamond.

Aaliyah moaned. "Not this again."

I didn't say a thing.

Veronique asked, "Not what again?" She looked at each of us. "Did I miss something?"

Aaliyah filled her in. "Diamond wants us all to share the lead. She wants a different lead in every city, but I'm staying in the back or y'all won't see me on that stage at all."

Veronique looked at me. "I don't want to sing the lead either," I said, not looking at Diamond at all. I hated when I had to side with one of my best friends over the other, but I wasn't skinny enough to be anybody's lead.

Slowly, Veronique turned like she was way pissed. She stared at Diamond like now she was ready to throw down, too. "You got a problem with me being the lead?"

"Not a problem. We just need to rotate."

I didn't want to see this turn into a fight, so I said, "I think we should just keep things the way they are, since we already won. So let's keep Vee at the lead and we'll keep on winning."

Why did I have to go and say anything? Diamond looked at me like she would never ever call me her best friend again.

"I agree with India," Aaliyah said, rescuing me.

Now all three of us looked at Diamond.

But this was Diamond Winters. And she was not about to be intimidated—not even by her three best friends.

"It's not fair that one person should get all the attention."

"Attention?" Veronique frowned. "Is that what this is about?"

"No, not attention. I want it to be fair for all of us."

"What's more fair than winning?" Aaliyah asked.

"Whatever, whatever." Diamond waved her hand in the air. "Like I said, I'm going to bring it up at rehearsal tomorrow. We'll see what Sybil has to say." Then she rolled her eyes and stomped away like we had done her wrong.

Five minutes ago, it had been good to be back with my best friends. But the good times had quickly gone bad. And the only times I could see ahead of us were hours filled with drama—nothing but straight drama.

chapter 11

Sometimes, being an only child was way cool.

Because I never had to share my parents with anyone—especially now that my dad wasn't playing football anymore. And because it was just me, I always got a lot of gifts for my birthday and for Christmas. And on weekends, we always did a lot of things I liked to do—like go to amusement parks or museums. And we went to a lot of plays, too.

That was all the good stuff, but there were lots of bad things, too. Like how I had to do all the chores in the house all by myself.

That's exactly what I was thinking about when I was loading the last plate from dinner into the dishwasher. I had already washed the pots. Tova didn't want any of her pots in the dishwasher. I never got that part—if you had a dishwasher, you shouldn't have to wash anything. But it was a rule, so I just had to live with it—at least that's what my daddy said.

"Are you almost finished?"

I looked up and saw my mom standing in the doorway, staring at me. The way she was looking, I could tell that I'd done something wrong. But I didn't know what.

"I rinsed all the plates before I put them in," I said, because that was the only thing I could have possibly done wrong.

"No, honey. You're fine." She stopped talking and walked around me, like she was doing an inspection or something.

I frowned. I wasn't really scared, because my mom just said I was fine. But the way she was looking at me—it felt the same as the way she'd looked a couple of weeks ago when she'd found out that I'd lied to Diamond's mother, Ms. Elizabeth, about Diamond spending the night with me. I'd been grounded for a week for trying to cover for Diamond so that she could spend the night with Jax.

I hadn't done anything like that since, so I didn't have a clue what this was all about.

Finally my mom smiled. "India, are you losing weight?"

It was only because she smiled that I nodded. I didn't think she would notice already. "I've kinda been on a diet," I said softly, trying to test out what she would think.

"Really?" She sounded way surprised. "At dinner, it didn't seem like—" She stopped. "Never mind. If you're dieting, that's a good thing." She took my hand. "You look terrific already."

"I do?" I couldn't stop grinning. It was because of the way my mother was looking at me. Like she was really feeling me.

"Yes, you do—you look fabulous! And I want to help you."

I didn't have any idea how she was going to help. Especially not with the way I was losing weight.

Then Tova explained. "I want to give you a little motivation, a little reward so that you'll keep going. On Saturday, let's go shopping!"

I was shaking my head before she even finished. "Oh, no, Tova. Not yet. I wanna lose some more weight first."

"I'm glad that you want to lose more, but we don't have to wait. We'll go shopping again, but I want to celebrate now." My mother put her arms around me and hugged me tight. "I'm so proud of you."

I couldn't remember another time when my mother made me feel so good. But still I told her, "Please, Tova. Can we wait just a few more weeks? I know I'll lose another twenty, maybe even thirty pounds by then."

My mother pulled back from me, and now her smile was gone, just a little. "Thirty pounds? In a couple of weeks?" She looked at me hard, like she was trying to see right through me. "That would be a lot of weight to lose in just a couple of weeks. And thirty pounds? You don't need to lose that much."

Okay, I needed to back up a little. Even though Tova wanted me to lose weight, she would have a fit if she found out how I was doing it. So I said, "You know what I mean. Not thirty pounds exactly. But it's just that I'm really serious about doing it this time, Tova. I'm really trying. And I'm gonna lose a lot of weight. So can we wait to go shopping? Please?"

"All right," my mother gave in. "I'll give you a little time." She kissed me on my forehead and walked with me out of the kitchen. "Do you have a lot of homework?"

"Not a lot. All of the teachers just really want us to start getting ready for finals. So I'm just gonna study. Especially French."

"*Oui, oui,*" Tova said, then laughed. She hugged me again. "I'll come in and say good night in a little while."

I could feel my mother watching me as I walked into my bedroom. After I closed the door, I leaned against it feeling all tingly. This was the best feeling, and I wanted it to just keep on. So I went into the bathroom and did my thing.

When I finished, I felt better than I usually did. I guess I was really getting used to throwing up. Or maybe it was just the good feeling that I got knowing that soon I was going to look like a diva for real. And then my mom would be really, really proud.

I sat at my desk and opened up my French book. But I couldn't stop smiling. I was feeling way, way good.

chapter 12

By the time we were in third grade we were BFFs. And in all of those years, I couldn't remember another time when there'd been so much drama between us. I mean, Diamond, she was always full of drama, but today, Veronique was caught up, too.

Since the blowup in front of our lockers yesterday, none of us had seen Diamond, except in class. She didn't come into the cafeteria for lunch today, and when we met in front of the school to ride to the church together for rehearsal, she never showed up.

But she was already here in the rec room when Veronique, Aaliyah, and I got here. She was holed up against the wall, just like she was now. Far away from us. Like she was way mad and didn't even want to share the same air with us.

The three of us stared at Diamond before Veronique said, "I can't stand this." She dropped her bag on the floor and marched over to her. "What's up?"

Diamond didn't even bother to look up. Just shrugged and

kept on flipping through her magazine. "I'm just waiting for Sybil to come so that I can make a few things clear."

Veronique crossed her arms. "A few things like what?"

Still not looking at Veronique, Diamond said, "We'll talk about it when Sybil gets here." And then she flicked her hand in the air like she was telling Veronique to go away. And Veronique did—she walked away mad!

"This is getting bad," I whispered to Aaliyah.

"Yeah. With the way this is going, we might not even make it to San Francisco. The Divine Divas just might be history."

Okay, now see—I wasn't feeling that. I know it was just a few days ago when I never wanted to perform on stage with my BFFs again, but now I had some hope. With the way this weight thing was going for me, I could be looking like a Divine Diva in the next couple of months, and I didn't want anyone messing it up.

"Do you really think we're going to break up?"

Aaliyah shrugged just as Sybil came strolling in.

"My ladies!" She was all happy, with a big smile and sparkling eyes. I shook my head as I looked at her. Her good mood would be over soon. "Did you all have a good holiday?" she asked, sounding like she had a lot of leftover Christmas cheer.

I was the only one who answered, "Yes."

The rest of my best friends all just kinda moaned. That was Sybil's first clue.

"What's up with y'all? I expected to see nothing but excitement when I walked in here. We'll be in San Francisco in six weeks." She said that as if she thought just the reminder would make everyone happy again.

But she didn't see a smile. And I surely wasn't going to say anything.

Sybil clapped her hands three times. "Okay, sit over here."

She motioned toward the bench. There was hardly room for three people, and with my butt, it made it even worse. I sat on the end so I could hang off the bench a bit, while my friends squeezed in.

"So, what's up?" Sybil asked. "Somebody want to fill me in?"

I put my head down.

"Well, I wanted to talk to you," Diamond began. "About the songs. And the leads." She stopped and looked at Veronique for a moment. But Veronique wouldn't look back at her.

Diamond continued. "I think we should take turns singing the lead. There are four performances and four of us. So that would give all of us a chance to be out front."

"Except," Aaliyah jumped in, "I don't want to be the lead." She stopped and looked at Sybil. "I keep telling her that, and if she keeps pushing it, I'm gonna quit."

Oh, no! Now my bestest wanted to break us up, too. This was getting way out of control.

Sybil's eyes were really narrow, but she still kept quiet.

That gave Veronique time to add her piece. "I don't know why we have to change anything," she said. "India and Aaliyah don't want to sing the lead. And"—she paused and looked at Diamond—"they think that I should be the one doing it because I have the best voice."

"Well, this whole group was my idea," Diamond snapped. "Nobody would be doing anything if I hadn't told you about the contest."

"What does that have to do with winning?" Veronique asked with all kinds of attitude in her voice. "Everything just needs to stay the same if we want to win this."

Diamond's eyes got wide, and she jumped up, right into Veronique's face. She was way, way mad. "Are you saying that we wouldn't win if I was doing the lead?"

Veronique did what she always did—she stood strong, not hardly backing down. "I'm just sayin' we don't need to trade in a winner for a loser."

For the first time, Sybil spoke, but it was more like a shout, "Okay, that's enough." Sybil held up her hands, stopping Diamond and Veronique. Good thing, because I was sure that next, there would be fists flying. "Everybody stop! You two," she demanded, pointing to Diamond and Veronique, "sit back down."

Sybil crossed her arms, stared, let us sit in the quiet, like she was just too through with everybody in, and everything about, the Divine Divas. "What is going on with you ladies? Where did all of this come from?"

Nobody said a thing.

"Okay, I must've missed something over the holidays because the last time we were together, the four of you were more than friends, you were sisters. So what happened?"

Again Sybil didn't get any kind of answer. From the corner of my eye, I peeked at my friends. Aaliyah was sitting next to me as if nothing big was going on. But on the other end of the bench, Veronique and Diamond sat like they were going to explode. Both of their faces were tight and hard. And their arms were folded, like they had to hold their hands back from slapping each other.

Sybil pulled up a stool and sat in front of us. Just like Pastor Ford used to do in our youth group when she was getting ready to give us a Christian lecture. "We need to talk." She paused for a minute as if she was trying to decide if she was still mad.

"When I was about seven years old . . ."

I stared at Sybil with my mouth wide open. I couldn't believe she was going to tell us one of those when-I-was-a-child stories. My father told me that kind of stuff all the time.

Daddy-talk was what Aaliyah and I called it. That was a long, long lecture that came from your just asking a little question. Like when I asked my dad for money, he would tell me how when he was a child he woke up at five every morning, without an alarm clock, and did all of his chores, and then checked his homework for the tenth time, and then walked thirteen miles to school, usually without shoes because his parents were too poor and couldn't afford shoes. And even when it was snowing, my dad still had to walk because that's what responsibility was all about.

A long time ago I figured out that my dad was telling a story because he grew up in Florida and it didn't even snow there. He just told me that so I wouldn't ask him for money.

I thought only old people made up stories like that. Sybil didn't seem to be that old, but this sure sounded like one of those long, drawn-out, sad stories.

"I was in Sunday school," Sybil continued, "and the lesson was about Jesus and His death. My teacher explained that the Pharisees had killed Jesus primarily because of one emotion." Sybil paused.

I wondered why she stopped, because her story was just beginning to get good. It didn't sound like one of my dad's lectures at all.

Sybil said, "Envy. Envy killed Jesus. Envy in the heart of the Pharisees. That's what my Sunday school teacher told us, and she showed us the scripture in the Bible. I didn't even know what envy was, but when I heard that, I knew I was never going to have any kind of envy in me. Because if envy could kill Jesus, I didn't even want to think about what it could do to me."

Okay, I got it. And I knew my best friends got it, too. Diamond and Veronique had to be feeling bad, because I was feeling bad and I hadn't even done anything.

"But envy is all through the Bible," Sybil said. "And it's all through the world. It's hard not to look around and wish that you had something someone else has. It's human nature. But what we're supposed to do as Christians is fight that human side and search for our spiritual side. Envy leads to coveting, wishing someone ill will. All of that is a sin."

Now Diamond looked like she was about to slide off the bench. For a moment, I wondered if she was gonna just fall to her knees and pray for forgiveness.

Diamond opened her mouth, but Sybil held up her hand.

"I'm not finished." Sybil paused. "There's something else I want to tell you. Do any of you know what humility means?"

Aaliyah's hand shot up like it always did in school, but Sybil didn't turn her head. She was staring straight at Veronique.

Now it wasn't just Diamond who seemed to want to disappear. Veronique said, "Yeah, humility means to be humble."

Sybil pressed, "What does being humble mean?"

"To be modest and unpretentious."

I raised my eyebrows a little bit. *Unpretentious?* That must've been one of those words that Diamond had studied in English.

"That's exactly what it means," Sybil said. "And not to be filled with pride. Do you think Jesus was humble?"

Okay, now see—Sybil was really pressing. She was making us all feel bad with these Jesus stories and Jesus questions.

But she just kept right on going. "Jesus was a great example of humility. Think about it. He was God. Even when He came to earth as man, He was still fully God. He could have done anything that He wanted to do. But God decided to come to earth as a servant.

"He came to teach us how to be good followers and good leaders, too. What you must all remember is that as believers, we're equal. We have different gifts and talents that have come from God, but He uses us all to fulfill His purpose. No one's gift is any better than the next person's. Does that make sense?"

I think we all felt too bad to speak. So we just nodded.

"Good. Now I'm done. This is your group. And I want everything that is part of the Divine Divas to always be the way you girls want it to be. So, tell me, what do you want to do now?"

At first there was no sound, because I think we all just wanted to go home and read our Bibles and pray. But then, all of a sudden, everybody was talking at the same time. Except for me.

Diamond was apologizing. Veronique was apologizing. Even Aaliyah, who hadn't done anything wrong, was saying that she was sorry, but that she still didn't want to sing the lead.

Sounding like she was about to cry, Diamond said to Veronique, "I think you should stay the lead."

But Veronique shook her head. "No, you were right. We should take turns. I'm not better than any of you. And I'm sorry, because I was acting like I thought I was." She bowed her head down a little bit. "I guess I got a little caught up."

"That's okay," Sybil said. "It happens to everyone. The good thing is when you can see it, then you can fix it." She turned to me and Aaliyah. "So you two really don't want to have anything to do with the lead?"

"No way," Aaliyah said, and I agreed. But then Aaliyah said, "But why don't Diamond and Vee share the lead?"

Veronique said, "That's a good idea. Diamond can sing the lead in San Francisco, and then when we win, I'll do it in New York, and then, when we win there, maybe we can figure out a way to both do it for the finals in Miami."

"Are you sure?" Diamond asked, now sounding a little excited.

With a grin, Veronique nodded. Then hugged Diamond. I don't know why we did, but Aaliyah and I hugged, too.

"Okay, so we're sistahs again, right?" Veronique asked as she reached for me and Aaliyah.

"Shoot, we were always sisters," Aaliyah said.

"Yeah," I said. "And we'll always be."

Diamond said, "We're more than sisters. We're the Divine Divas."

And then we hugged in a circle.

"Ladies, did you forget about me?"

We laughed as Sybil joined our hug circle.

"Okay, it's time to get to work. We have to rework the vocals and really get the words to this song down because Turquoise will be back next week to incorporate the choreography."

It felt like everything was normal again when we stood around the piano. I was glad this drama was over, but there was still one thing—I really wasn't sure about Diamond being the lead. Veronique and Aaliyah were way, way better than me and Diamond when it came to singing. If we really wanted to win, Veronique needed to be singing right up front.

But I wasn't gonna say a word. If this would keep the peace, then I was all for it. This was Diamond's problem now. She wanted the lead—she got it. And anyway, I had too many other things to be thinking about—like how I was gonna look in San Francisco. I was getting excited because I knew that no matter what it took, I was gonna look good on that stage, too.

chapter 13

I peeked under the comforter, then looked back to make sure my bedroom door was closed before I pulled the scale from under my bed.

Holding my breath, I watched the needle move. And then it stopped. Right around 180. My eyes opened way wide. I couldn't believe it.

It had only been three weeks since Jill had told me the secret, and already I had lost twenty pounds. I really was eating a whole lot less than before. And it helped that I had gotten rid of my stash—even though I was still dropping in on the golden arches to pick up a few apple pies a couple of times a week.

But what was really working for me was the throwing up. I wished Jill had told me about this a long time ago. I would have been much happier by now.

"India!" I heard my mom call me from down the hall.

Oh, my God. I was still standing on top of the scale. I kicked the metal circle back under the bed and was standing at attention when Tova opened my door.

"Hi! How was the dinner?" I decided that if I asked her about her night right away, she wouldn't be wondering what I'd been doing in my room.

"It was just fabulous." My mom held her hands as if she was posing for the paparazzi or something. "We raised a ton of scholarship money."

I grinned. My mother was always so happy when she talked about the work she did to help kids in foster care. I was really proud of her, though sometimes I didn't think that she knew that.

"Well, I just wanted to tell you that I was home." My mother stared at me for an extra moment. "You look really good, honey," she said, her eyes still on me. "You're still losing weight."

The way she looked at me made me smile so hard my cheeks hurt. "I think I've lost a lot. But I'm not for sure." I didn't know why I told that lie. I guess I just wanted to play it cool. That's why I still wore all my big skirts and tops. I didn't want anyone to get suspicious; I didn't want anyone or anything to mess me up.

Suddenly, my mother grabbed my hand and almost dragged me into her bedroom. In her bathroom, she pulled out the scale that I'd been sneaking and using before I'd bought my own. "Let's take a peek," my mom said, so excited.

If I didn't already know, I might not have wanted to be weighed. But I took off my shoes and hopped right on.

Like two seconds later, my mother was clapping her hands. "Oh, my goodness, honey. You're one hundred and eighty pounds. What did you weigh the last time we went to the doctor?"

I said, "Almost two hundred," like I was proud of that number. I was proud—now that I didn't weigh 200 pounds anymore.

Tova hugged me, as if I'd just won something. "That is

terrific." She grabbed my hand and dragged me again. This time, I didn't even have a clue where we were going—until we stopped right in front of the family room. Where my dad was reading his newspaper. He looked up when he heard us.

"Marvin, look at India. I am so proud of her."

Before my dad even dropped the newspaper, he was smiling. "Well, I'm always proud of her, but what specifically are you proud of, sweetheart?"

Tova stood back and beamed at me, like she had done all the work. "Just look at her."

My dad looked at my mom, and you could tell by the way he frowned that he had no idea what she was talking about. "Yeah, she's beautiful, isn't she? But I've always thought that. From the day she was born."

"Of course she's beautiful." My mother threw her hands in the air as if my dad was stating the obvious. "But that's not what I'm talking about. Look at her!"

My father stared at me for a moment, then grinned. "Oh, I know what this is about. You got all As on your finals!"

I giggled.

"My daughter—beautiful and brilliant."

I laughed a little harder. I wasn't the dumbest kid on the block, but I'd never gotten all As in my whole life. My dad must've had me confused with my bestest.

"Daddy, we don't have finals till next week."

"Guess again, Marvin." My mother wasn't about to give up.

My dad stared at me some more. "Oh, I know. It's about the Divine Divas." He started nodding, like he was absolutely sure he was right this time. "They've decided that you girls are so good they're calling off the whole competition and just declaring the Divine Divas the winners!" He held his hands in the air like he had just scored a touchdown. "I knew it. My daughter—beautiful, brilliant, and a bona fide star."

I laughed some more and my dad did, too. But Tova didn't.

"Marvin, stop playin'." She put her hands on her hips. "I can't believe you can't see it." And then she took a deep breath, like she was about to make a big announcement. "India's lost twenty pounds!"

My father was still smiling, but not as much as before. "Well, that's good, sweetheart," he said and then kinda eased back in his chair, like he wasn't sure what to say next. He looked at me harder, and I could tell that for the first time he noticed that I had lost some weight. "So, you've been dieting?"

I knew my dad wouldn't like that, so I just shrugged. "Not really dieting. I'm just trying to eat a little better."

Uh-oh. That was the wrong answer. Now my dad was looking at me so hard, I wouldn't have been surprised if he was reading my brain. I couldn't read his, but I knew what he was thinking about—those five slices of pizza I'd had at dinner. Since Tova hadn't been there, I'd thought I could have as many as I'd wanted because my dad never cared about how much I ate.

But now I knew he had to be wondering how eating all of that pizza was eating better.

So I decided I needed to say a little bit more. "Most of the time, I'm pretty good," I added, hoping that would explain it to him.

Slowly, my dad nodded. "That's good," he said, like he was trying to convince himself.

Then it kinda got really weird in the room. Just quiet. With my mom looking at me and my dad looking at my mom. And I was looking at both of them.

"Okay, I'm going back to study." I was already backing out of the family room. I walked down the hallway pretending to be heading to my bedroom, but I stopped right at the corner.

Where my mom and dad couldn't see me. And I couldn't see them. But I could hear every word.

My dad said, "Tova, did you take her to that doctor?"

"Of course not. I wouldn't do that after you said you didn't want her to go."

"I'm just checking, because I don't know how she lost twenty pounds."

"She told you, she's been eating better. I can't believe you didn't notice."

I held my breath and wished I could see my father's face. He had to still be thinking about all of that pizza.

"Well, I don't want her losing any more," he said. "She's just a kid; I told you, I don't want her worrying about her weight."

"That's where you're wrong, Marvin. She's not a kid. India's almost sixteen. She's a young woman. And in this world, women are treated harshly if they're overweight. I don't want that for India."

That was when I tiptoed into my bedroom.

Boy, this could be trouble. If my father suspected anything, he would go searching. And if he found out what I was doing, he would shut my weight loss program down for good.

I had to be more careful. From now on, I had to act like I was on a diet all the time. I wouldn't eat anything in front of anybody!

That was my new plan—I couldn't take any more risks!

chapter 14

I felt like one of those kids on that old TV show that still ran on cable—*Beverly Hills, 90210.*

My mother had me marching up and down the three famous blocks of Rodeo Drive, going in and out of all the stores like Anthropologie, and Bebe, and Guess. And I was just loving it.

There had never been a time in my whole life when I'd gone shopping with my mother and had been happy about it. No matter what we were shopping for or when we went shopping, it was always way horrible. Like the last time we went to buy new clothes for school. My mom took me out to this outlet mall near Palm Springs, and we went into all of these cool stores. But no matter where we went, nothing fit me. Finally, my mom took me into one of those big-girl shops. I was so humiliated. But what was way worse was the way Tova looked at me that whole day. Like she'd never been so disappointed about anything in her entire life.

But not today. Tova was grinning, and it started last night at dinner.

"I think you deserve a reward for making it through your first semester as a sophomore," my mom said just as I scraped the last bit of gravy off my plate. I had long ago finished my little piece of chicken.

"Really?" I was so glad to have something else to think about instead of those sweet potatoes that were still piled in that dish in the middle of the table. I'd been staring at them for like an hour and I wanted some more so bad. But for the last week, I was trying really hard not to eat too much in front of my mom, and especially my dad. It had to look like I was really losing weight the regular way.

"What kind of reward?" I finally asked my mother when I stopped staring at those sweet potatoes.

"Hmmm, I was thinking about something like," she paused and grinned, "hanging out on Rodeo."

My eyes opened way wide. "Rodeo *Drive?*"

Tova nodded, and I had never been so happy. My mother wanted to take me shopping to the best stores in the country.

But then my dad asked, "If you're taking her shopping for making it through sophomore year, don't you think we should wait until she actually takes her finals next week?"

"With the way India's been studying"—my mom paused, waved her fork in the air, and I stared at the little piece of chicken that was dangling on the end—"her grades will be good, right, honey?"

I nodded. "I'm still studying really hard." I turned to my father. "I know I won't have all As, but I'm not going to get anything lower than a B."

"See?" my mother said. "Our brilliant daughter deserves a reward."

There was no way my father could say no after that.

He smiled. "Okay, we'll just call this a pre-reward. And

when we get your report card, if it's not good, you're going to have to take everything back."

My dad was still smiling, but I knew he could have been serious. I wouldn't have been surprised if I had one C on that report card, my father might have marched me right back to every store and gotten his money back. Daddy was way serious when it came to good grades. Much tougher than my mother, who worried much more about how I looked than what I studied in school.

"Great!" my mother said. "We'll go tomorrow and have a Saturday girls' day out."

I had a feeling that this reward didn't have anything to do with my grades. This was about how almost every day my mom weighed me and watched how I kept dropping the pounds. Tova was way thrilled.

And so was I. This morning—exactly one week after Tova first weighed me—I was down another seven pounds. My mom couldn't wait to take me shopping.

"Oh, my gosh!" my mother said when I stepped out of the Guess dressing room. "That's a fourteen." She tugged at the jacket. "And the pants and the jacket are too big."

I looked in the mirror. This jean suit rocked. But the best part was that it *was* too big.

Tova asked the sales associate to get a smaller size. And when I slipped right into a size twelve, there was not a happier girl on the planet. Nobody could tell me that I didn't look good.

I stared in the mirror and tried to see myself on the stage next to my BFFs now. I could almost imagine it.

I turned around so that I could check out the back. Yeah, I did look good. But I was still a size twelve. That was definitely way big for any kind of diva.

I still had a lot of work to do.

chapter 15

Diamond slammed her locker door so hard, it woke me up from the daydream I was having standing right there in the school hallway.

"So are you guys ready to roll?" Diamond asked.

Aaliyah looked at her watch. "We have almost two hours before practice."

Diamond swung her designer bag over her shoulder. "But it never hurts to put in extra time. And anyway, I wanted to show you guys some steps I came up with last night."

"What's wrong with the steps we have now?" Veronique frowned. "Turquoise already choreographed everything."

"I know, but this is our show and we need to add our own flava."

Aaliyah said, "I think Turquoise's flavor is just fine."

"Yeah, but I was thinking that at the end . . ."

Diamond kept talking, but I had stopped listening. No doubt I loved her like a sister, but dang, she was taking this being the lead way too seriously. Ever since she took over, she

91

was acting like she was Beyoncé and we were just her backup singers.

But right now, I didn't feel like thinking about Diamond or even the Divine Divas. There was something way bigger on my mind. Something that I'd been thinking about all day and had even dreamed about last night.

"Well, I'll see the steps later," Aaliyah said. "I'm going to study hall so that I won't be up so late tonight."

"I'm going with you." Veronique grabbed her backpack from her locker. "Maybe you can help me with this one problem I'm having in geometry, 'cause I'm trying to ace this class."

Then all three of my friends turned to me.

"Ah, I have to run an errand."

"What kind of errand?" Diamond asked.

"Something for my mother."

"Oh, okay, I'll go with—"

And before my bestest could say anything more, I shouted, "That's okay, Aaliyah."

The way my BFFs looked at me, you would have thought I'd stolen something.

"I'm just sayin', you just said you didn't want to be up late tonight. And Vee just said she needs your help. And what I have to do is no biggie. And I'm . . . just dropping something off . . . at home," I stuttered, trying to find the right lie.

They were still giving me that what's-up-with-you look, but finally, Veronique and Aaliyah headed toward the study room and I left the building with Diamond.

"You know, we really need to put in the extra practice time," Diamond said as we stepped outside. "San Fran isn't going to be easy."

I couldn't believe she was saying that. From the beginning, Diamond was way sure that we were going to win the whole thing. Now I wondered if she'd come up with the extra practice because she wasn't so sure. And maybe she wasn't so sure because she was now the lead.

"You don't still think we're going to win this?" I asked.

"I think we are, but we've got to start behaving like professionals."

Okay, now see—this lead thing was getting to her. That was the only way to explain why she was beginning to sound like Aaliyah.

Diamond said, "Do you know how often Kobe Bryant or Shaquille O'Neal or Dwayne Wade practices? Even though they're stars, they stay on top of their game by practicing. That's what we need to do."

I couldn't figure out why she was comparing us to some basketball players. That must have been leftover stuff from when she and Jax were a couple.

"Well, I want us to win, too," I said. "And after today, I promise I'll practice all the time, every day if you want."

"That's what I'm talking about." She stopped, looked me up and down. "You're really lookin' good, India."

It made me way happy that everyone was beginning to notice.

"Are you sure you're not on a diet?"

"Not a diet. Not really. Just trying to be more healthy," I said, staying with my story.

"Well, it shows. You look great." Then she bounced down the steps. "Holla."

I turned and walked in the opposite direction, as if I was going home. And as I moved, I thought about what Diamond had said. Everyone was beginning to notice how much weight I'd lost. And it did seem to be coming off faster now that I *was* trying to eat better—most of the time.

I walked two blocks, then stopped. Looked up. And there

it was. What I had been dreaming about and thinking about for days now.

The golden arches. And they looked way better in person than they did in my dreams.

This was the best hamburger I had ever tasted. It was even better than the first double-cheeseburger I had just finished a couple of minutes ago.

I took another huge bite of my hamburger, then grabbed a couple of fries and stuffed it all into my mouth. I sure hoped God had all of this good stuff in heaven.

I don't know why, but all I had dreamed about last night was these golden arches. And then today, everywhere I went everything looked like a hamburger or smelled like French fries. Even this morning, my toothpaste tasted like a milkshake. I would have never been able to sleep tonight if I hadn't done this hamburger thing today.

But the more I ate, the worse I felt. It was always like this after I ate a lot. I guess it was because I felt guilty when I did this. Especially today, since I hadn't lost any weight in the past couple of days. I was still just hanging around 173.

But even though I felt bad, it was like I couldn't help it. I needed to have these hamburgers today.

I stuffed the last bit into my mouth and decided that I could use just one more. But then I glanced at my watch. There was no time for any more food. I'd have to get into the bathroom right now if I wanted to make it to church on time. I had to be quick, 'cause Sybil had a fit if we were ever late: "Stars, divas, celebrities—all of these people have one thing in common— they take care of business. And that's what I expect from you ladies. I will not tolerate lateness."

I didn't feel like hearing that speech.

I grabbed the empty wrappers and jumped up from the chair, but my stomach squeezed and tightened like it was really mad at me, stopping me cold. A couple of seconds later, it was gone.

It still took me a few moments before I could take a step or two. I was afraid that the pain was going to come back. But after a while, I was able to walk regular.

It was probably just because I hadn't eaten here in a long time—like for a couple of weeks. And I'd probably just eaten the best food in the whole wide world too fast.

Knocking on the bathroom door, I was way glad that this was one of those restaurants with a single bathroom. I hated when there was more than one stall—I was always so afraid that someone might come in and hear me doing my thing. That would be a way big disaster.

I clicked the lock, dropped my bag to the floor, and looked at my watch again. Just a couple of minutes and I'd be out.

Getting in position, I pulled my hair back, leaned over the toilet and did what I had to do. Then I pushed myself up. "Ahhhh . . . ," I moaned and fell right back to my knees.

My stomach squeezed again, this time real tight.

"Ahhhhhhh . . ." I pressed my hand against my stomach, praying that would stop some of the ache.

But it didn't go away. The pain just kept on coming. And it was way worse than before.

I couldn't breathe. I started to sweat. My heart was pounding hard and fast. I felt like I was dying.

I didn't know what to do, but I had to do something. I couldn't just die on the bathroom floor under the golden arches.

"Help," I yelled out. But my stomach hurt so bad that my yell was just a tiny little cry. Someone standing right next to me probably wouldn't have heard me.

"Help," I tried again. But it wasn't any louder. I was just going to die—at the age of fifteen!

That thought gave me a little more strength. "Help!"

But no one came.

Even though I hadn't flushed the toilet yet, I rested my head on the seat, not caring even a little bit about the icky smell. I couldn't care about that since I was dying.

I closed my eyes, held my stomach, and started counting, wondering how long it would take for death to come.

But then by the time I got to twenty, the pain started to go away. Just a little, at first. And then, more and more. I kept counting, praying that by the time I got to one hundred I would be better. And better came. Right around seventy-nine.

But I didn't make a move. Just thinking about how I'd been hurting made me stay right there on the bathroom floor for a couple more minutes. When everything inside of me seemed normal, I got up, flushed the toilet, and rinsed off my face and mouth.

What just happened? I wondered as I looked into the mirror. I had never in my whole life felt any kind of pain like that.

I just ate too fast, I told myself again. That had to be it.

I looked at my watch. Dang! I was late now for sure. A Sybil lecture was definitely coming.

As I dashed out of the restaurant, I kept thinking about what Sybil was going to say. I needed to be ready with some kind of excuse, but I couldn't think of anything. Except for the truth—I could tell her that she was lucky to have me there because I almost died.

Maybe she would go easy on me once I told her that.

chapter 16

I tried to open my mouth, but not one sound came out.

It was probably because of the way my stomach was turning and twisting. Like it was trying to sing its own song or do its own dance. The pain just wouldn't go away.

"India!" Sybil clapped her hands. "Pay attention! What's wrong with you today?"

I crossed my feet one in front of the other and moved with my friends. Snapping my fingers, I did that pirouette that Diamond added and almost fell to the floor.

I could feel Sybil's angry eyes on me. She'd been on my case from the moment I'd walked into rehearsal.

"Unless you were in a meeting with God or Pastor, I don't want to hear it."

So I hadn't bothered to tell her that I'd almost died. Instead, I'd just gotten in line with my friends and started dancing like I hadn't been twenty minutes late.

But the cramps had come back. Not as bad as before, but enough to make me just want to lie down on the floor and fold myself in half. I should've told Sybil that I was sick and then maybe I would've been home right now, tucked away in my bed.

"India!" Sybil yelled again. "Keep up!" She paused for a moment. "You know what? Let's take ten. But just ten." She looked straight at me and added, "And when we come back, let's have it together." She tried to just strut out of the room, but the way her shoulders were tight and her eyes were staring directly ahead, I knew she was way mad.

"Wow," and then Aaliyah took a sip from her water bottle. "What's gotten up her butt?" My bestest's eyes were watching the door where Sybil had just stomped away.

"It's India," Diamond said.

The way she said my name, I thought for a moment that my friend was mad at me, too, because Diamond was taking this contest so much more seriously now. But when I looked at her, she had this big ole grin on her face.

"What's up with you?" Diamond asked me.

"Nothing," I said before I leaned against the wall and slid down until I plopped right onto the floor.

"Well, first you were late—"

"That wasn't my fault."

"And now you're acting like you can't concentrate," Diamond finished.

That's because I'm sick, was what I wanted to scream. But I just kept quiet like I always did. I knew I was pouting, but I couldn't help it. It wasn't fair—Sybil was picking on me.

"I know what's wrong with you," Veronique piped in. "It's all the weight you've lost. You're just getting used to moving around being so much lighter," she kidded. "How much have you lost anyway?"

"I don't know." I shrugged. "I wasn't really trying to lose

weight." When Aaliyah raised her eyebrows at me, I added, "I just wanted to get healthy."

"Well, whatever you've done, you done it good, my sistah."

"Thanks." I couldn't even show Veronique that I was happy, even though I was way thrilled on the inside. But my rumbling stomach kept all of my smiles away.

"By the way," Veronique said to Diamond, "those steps you added, I have to admit, they were tight. We'll be mad different from everyone else on the stage doing all that crunk and other hip-hop stuff. We'll still be cool, but elegant, you know?"

Diamond laughed. "See, I tried to tell you guys." And while Diamond chatted with Veronique, Aaliyah came over to where I was resting.

"So," she began, "are you going to tell me what's going on?" Before I could say anything, she added, "And don't pretend it's nothing, because I can tell it's something. And I won't stop until I find out."

Okay, now see—this could be bad. Aaliyah could be as determined as my father; if there was something going on, she *would* find out. I guess it was because her dad was one of the head honchos with the police department. Being a detective was probably way deep in her blood.

"I'm just not feeling well," I said, thinking that with my bestest it was much safer to stick close to the truth. "My stomach hurts."

"Does that have anything to do with the diet that you're *not* on?"

"No, it's not the diet," I responded with a lower voice, hoping that she would start whispering, too. "And come on, Aaliyah. You know why I don't want Diamond and Vee to know. I don't want them making fun of me."

"Who would make fun of you, India?" Her eyebrows were bunched together like she thought what I was saying was crazy.

"And even if they were going to make fun of you before, there's no way anybody could do that now. Trust, Diamond and Vee would never tease you about this."

"I know they won't because I'm not going to tell them." And without saying it, I knew she'd gotten the message that she was still sworn to secrecy.

She shrugged. "I'm not gonna give you up." She stopped, looked me up and down.

This was one of those moments when I wished I had brain radar. I just had to know what she was thinking. My bestest was the only one who hadn't said anything about how good I looked.

"Just be careful," Aaliyah whispered and squeezed my hand right when Sybil came back in the room.

I wanted to figure out what she thought I needed to be careful about, but I couldn't think about that now. All I could do was push my body up and pray that I would be able to dance, even though my stomach was still acting like it was a gymnast.

Then Sybil saved my life. "We're gonna stop here tonight," she said. She folded her arms. "Divas, you still need a lot of work, so between practices, find a way to work it out at home. Please!"

"Yes," we all responded together like we were singing the chorus to a song.

I grabbed my bag, grateful that in twenty minutes, I would be crawling into my soft bed and making this pain go away.

"India, can I see you for a minute?" Sybil called from across the room while we were all packing up.

Just when I was starting to feel better. But with Sybil wanting to see me, I knew better was still a little ways away.

Sybil wasn't a yeller, but I wouldn't have blamed her if she'd started screaming at me. So before she could say a word, I said, "I'm sorry about today. I'm just not feeling well, and I should have told you at the beginning."

Sybil crossed her arms and stared at me as if she was looking right through me. And then, in a gentle voice, she asked, "Are you okay, India?"

I wondered if she had just heard what I said. "Yeah, I'm fine, except that my stomach hurts a little. I think it was something I ate." At least that was the truth. None of this would have happened if I hadn't eaten those super-size hamburgers so fast.

Sybil kept looking at me, her eyes on my eyes. And without breaking her stare, she took my hand.

I smiled. Okay, so now I did feel a little better. She wasn't so mad. And the soft way she held my hand, I could tell that she wanted me to know that. I would just promise her that I wouldn't be sick again.

Then Sybil's expression changed, and I wondered why she was frowning. I looked down so that I could see what she saw. And I almost screamed.

I stood frozen for a moment as we both stared at my hands. At my fingernails. And the black around the edges. Not totally black. Kind of dark gray.

I had noticed that a little the other day, but they looked way worse now than they did in my bedroom.

"India."

I snatched my hand back, but I don't know why. It was way too late.

"What's wrong with your—"

"That's the dye," I interrupted her. "From the jewelry I make. I've been working with the dye and I guess I need to get something to take it off my hands . . . better."

"India," Sybil started and then stopped.

I stood there, hoping I wasn't shaking. There was a big ole

lump in my throat, and I wondered if it came from all the lies I was telling.

Sybil continued, staring again right into my eyes. "India, you know you can talk to me."

"I know, but there's nothing to talk about."

"I'm concerned—your fingers, your stomach."

Oh, no. If Sybil suspected, then she would say something to Pastor Ford. Or even my parents. "Sybil, I'm fine really. My stomach was hurting because of what I ate. I hadn't had a hamburger in a long time and I got sick."

She stared at me longer, making my heart pound so hard, I forgot how much my stomach was hurting.

"Okay," she said finally. "But India, if you ever need to talk, I'm always here for you."

I nodded like it was no big deal, but with the way she was still looking at me, I was having a hard time breathing. I ran across the room to where my friends stood.

"My dad just called. He was on his way home anyway, so he'll stop by and pick us up," Aaliyah announced. "He'll be here in five."

I looked over my shoulder, and Sybil was still standing there with her arms folded, staring. "Okay, let's wait outside."

I tucked my hands into my pockets so that no one else would notice my fingers. I had to get home. Get home quick and give Jill a call.

chapter 17

So, let me get this straight, you've been throwing up three times a day?"

I heard the shock in my cousin's voice as I pressed the telephone closer to my ear. Even though my mom and dad were out at some fund-raiser tonight and I was home alone, I still kept my voice low, not wanting to take any chances.

"I've been throwing up more than three times," I whispered. "I do it every time I eat."

Now I could almost see Jill frowning with the way she asked, "Well, how many times do you eat, Indy?"

Okay, now see—she hurt my feelings just by the way she asked that. I knew what my cousin was thinking—how it was totally ridiculous to eat even three times in one day. But though I was starting to get mad, I couldn't. At least not before Jill told me what I needed to know.

"Indy?" she called me again.

I guess I was taking too long to respond, but it was hard to answer her question. I really didn't know how many times

I ate in one day. If you just counted the meals that would be just three times. But what about every time I had a cupcake or a bag of potato chips or even a milkshake. Every time I ate anything, I tried to throw up. That was probably nine, ten times a day.

"I don't know how many times," I said, finally answering her question. "I just know that it's a lot more than three."

"And you're still losing weight even though you're eating like that?"

I couldn't believe my cousin said that. My feelings were like on the edge of hurt now. "Yeah, I'm still losing a lot." I got up from my bed and looked into my mirror. Whenever I did that, I felt better. Sometimes it even made me want to eat less and throw up more.

"Wow, that's a lot of purging, Indy. I only do it at night, after dinner, when I eat a lot."

I eat a lot all the time was what I should have said. But I just listened, waiting for her to give me some good advice. I'd called Jill the moment I'd gotten home from that disaster at rehearsal with Sybil. Even though I was safe in my house, I was still trembling—especially when I looked at my fingers.

"You've got to be throwing up an awful lot for it to turn your fingers black. That's like so gross."

Didn't she think I knew that? But it wasn't any more gross than throwing up. And it really wasn't so gross now that I'd lost twenty-five pounds in just a little over a month.

"So what are you going to do?" she asked me.

"I don't know. That's why I was calling you."

"I don't know anything about that, Indy. All I know is to drink ginger ale if your stomach starts hurting."

I frowned. "Why?"

"I think it has something to do with the acid settling your stomach. That's just something good to know if it happens to you. But the fingers thing . . ." She paused. "Ewwww, gross."

I wished she would stop saying that.

"But I got your back. I'll look it up on the 'Net, ask around in school, and make some calls, too."

Okay, now see—that was enough to make me throw up without using my fingers. "Who're you gonna call?" I said, feeling a little bit panicked. "You can't call anyone who might talk to Daddy or Tova."

"Indy, you live in Inglewood—"

"Ladera. And what does that have to do—"

"We live in the Hollywood Hills. None of my friends' parents know Aunt Tova and Uncle Marvin. Believe that."

If I didn't need her so much, I would have hung up right now.

"And anyway, I'm not gonna talk to any grown-ups about this. Just some of my friends. And their friends. Someone will know what to do. One thing's for sure—stop using your fingers to throw up, especially since you do it so much. Use a toothbrush or something—some of my friends do that. And I'll find out how to get that yucky stuff off your fingers! Ewwww. Gross!"

I was pretty mad at Jill by the time I hung up. And if I didn't need her so much, I would have told her that. But I wasn't going to say a thing. I never said anything to anybody, no matter how mad I got.

I leaned back on the bed. My stomach still felt like there was a boxing match going on inside. But even though I ached, my mind was really on Jill. And hoping that she would call back soon, because I was starting to get scared.

All I wanted to do was lose some weight, and now everyone was on my tail. They didn't even know it, but so many people were so close to finding out that I had a secret.

I had to do everything I could to make sure my secret never got out. If anyone uncovered it, I would never get to 150 pounds. That's what I'd decided I wanted to weigh in San Francisco. I was desperate to reach that and I couldn't let anything get in my way—not my dad, not my bestest, not Sybil, not my fingernails, and not even my stomach, which was still treating me like a punching bag.

No matter what it took, I was going to be a skinny diva.

chapter 18

"Let's go shopping!" I said. And then I cracked up with the way my best friends looked at me. Like I was a visitor from another planet or something. I didn't know why they were trippin' like that.

We'd been off from school for two days and we were all bored. There was absolutely nothing to do at my house, although my dad told me that when he was a kid, he didn't have all the TVs and computers and Playstations that we have now. But that little bit of history lesson didn't have anything to do with me. After two days at home all by myself, I was way bored. And I was eating way too many snacks. I had to get out of my house, and my best friends felt the same way.

Diamond complained that she couldn't find anything to watch on TV because her parents refused to pay for more than the one-hundred-channel basic cable. Veronique complained that it was horrible sharing their small apartment with her four younger brothers because they were always in her way. And Aaliyah complained that in today's times, the school officials were doing us kids a "gross injustice" because they had us out of school too much. Even though I couldn't get with Aaliyah on that injustice stuff, I was still feeling her boredom.

So we'd all met here at Starbucks to hang out and find something to do before our rehearsal tonight. But it seemed that now that I'd come up with this idea, no one had anything to say.

"What?" I asked them when they kept staring.

Aaliyah took a last sip of her Frappuccino before she said, "*You* wanna go shopping?"

"Yeah." I shrugged. "What's wrong with that?"

"Well then, let's raise up out of here!" Diamond was already pushing her chair back.

"But you hate shopping," Veronique said as if I needed to be reminded. "That's why we'd stopped doing it together all the time—because of you."

"Why're y'all trying to talk her out of it?" Now Diamond was standing at the door. "Let's go."

I jumped up behind Diamond so that Veronique and Aaliyah would know that I was serious. When we got outside, Veronique started walking west, and Diamond frowned.

"Where are you going? The bus stop is this way."

"If we go to Fox Hills, we can just walk down there and then take the bus straight to church," Veronique said.

Diamond crossed her arms and stood like she wasn't about to get with that idea. "Y'all know I don't hang at the Fox anymore. It's only Beverly Hills for me." She turned around and headed toward the bus, but when we didn't follow her, Diamond came back to us, stomping all the way. "How are we gonna call ourselves divas and shop anyplace besides Beverly Hills? We're *divas*. We gotta hang out and shop with the stars."

We still stared at her, but an hour later, we were strolling through the Beverly Center exactly the way Diamond wanted.

"Look at those jeans!" Diamond exclaimed as she pointed to a pair in the window of Headed for the Stars. She grabbed Veronique's hand and rushed into the store. Aaliyah and I just followed them.

"They are to die for!" Diamond held up the rhinestone-studded pants.

"Not to die for," Aaliyah said, holding up her own pair, "but they are cute."

"Trust and know," Veronique agreed. "Look at these stars." She turned her pants to the side to check out the rhinestones running down both seams. "We should all get a pair."

"And you know what would be fierce?" There was nothing but excitement in Diamond's voice. "If we all got a pair and then wore them when we fly up to San Fran. We'll get off the plane looking like the divas we are."

At first, Aaliyah nodded like she agreed, but then she looked at the tag. "Do you know how much these cost?"

I peeked at the price. Eighty dollars. That was way more than I'd ever spent on jeans. Your basic denim for big girls didn't cost that much. But how could they? They weren't anywhere near this cute.

Diamond said, "Come on, y'all. You gotta pay to play, you gotta buy to be fly."

"It'll be more like die to be fly if my mama finds out I paid eighty dollars for a pair of pants," Veronique said.

"But you said the money you were earning was for the Divine Divas," Diamond said.

"Yeah, but—"

"No buts. When we wear these, we'll be divas for sure." Veronique was still frowning when Diamond added, "Come on, at least let's try them on."

109

Aaliyah was still holding her pair. "Trying them on can't hurt, but I'm with you, Vee. They're too expensive."

"I wish y'all would stop thinking about money."

"Spoken like the girl who has her parents' credit cards," Veronique said.

"Exactly! Which is why I can call the judge, tell her we're getting these jeans for the show, and she'll let me charge all four pairs."

"I can buy my own," Aaliyah said.

"Whatever, whatever, let's just do this."

My three best friends were already walking to the dressing room before Aaliyah turned back and remembered me. Then, just like that, their faces became all droopy. Like they felt sorry for me.

"Oh . . . Indy . . ."

I said, "Can y'all help me find my size? I think I need . . . a ten."

Diamond was back, standing by my side before all the words had come out of my mouth. "Get out," she shouted. "You cannot be wearing a ten!"

Okay, now see—a couple of weeks ago, my feelings would have been way hurt. But that was when I was nothing more than a fat girl. Now I knew Diamond was just being Diamond. The first thing she thought was the first thing she said.

I was grinning when I said, "I think I'm a ten."

"I didn't know you'd lost that much weight, my sistah."

"That's because she's still wearing all those big clothes." Diamond was already pulling pants out of the stack that was piled high on the table. "Here." She handed me a pair of tens and then pushed me into the fitting room in front of her.

My friends were still laughing and talking through the walls as we took off our clothes. But in the privacy of my fitting stall, my heart was pounding hard. A size ten—if I could really get into these . . .

I put one leg into the pants, then took a breath before I stepped into the other. And then I got scared. What if the ten didn't fit? That would be way embarrassing. I'd have to make up something. Like I didn't like the rhinestones. Or I thought stars were stupid.

I closed my eyes, took in a deep breath, then pulled the denim up, and up and up. Until I buttoned them around my waist. My eyes were opened way wide when I finally looked in the mirror. They fit! And there was even a little bit of room!

I was so excited that I had to use both of my hands to cover my mouth. I felt like laughing, and crying, and screaming, all at the same time.

But all I did was stand still and stare at myself in the mirror. Then I grabbed the scrunchy from my purse that I used to tie my hair back while we were rehearsing. I flipped my hair into a ponytail on the top of my head like Aaliyah had shown me.

I turned from side to side, admiring my hair in the mirror. I had to admit, I did like this style—especially since my face looked way skinnier than it did before.

"India!" Diamond banged on my door. "Let me see."

I took another breath, then stepped into the hallway.

"Oh, my God!" Diamond screamed so loud that Veronique and Aaliyah came running out of their rooms. "You look something fierce. I guess because we see you every day, I didn't realize how skinny you were now!"

I couldn't stop grinning.

"How did you do it, my sistah? How did you lose all that weight?"

"You know, like I told you before. I just started eating healthier." I made sure my back was to Aaliyah when I said that. I didn't want to see her face.

"Now we've *got* to get these pants," Diamond said, looking at Veronique and Aaliyah. "It's the first time ever that India will be able to wear the same thing as us."

I had to suck it up again and remember how Diamond's mind and mouth worked. But although she hurt my feelings a little, she wasn't lying. This *was* the first time ever that I was able to look almost as cute as my friends.

"Look how good we *all* look," Diamond continued, pleading her case.

The four of us turned to the mirror, and right there in the hall of the fitting room, we primped and posed like we were junior Tovas.

"Ooohhh, let's do this." Diamond pushed us all to the side, then she walked down the long hall, one foot in front of the other, like she was on a runway in Europe.

We laughed and clapped before Veronique took her turn and Aaliyah followed. Then, standing at the other end, my three friends waited for me.

Just a few weeks ago, I would have rather died than do anything like this—even playing around with my friends.

But in these size tens, I felt as cute as they looked. And I'd never, ever in my whole life felt that way before.

I put one foot forward on our imaginary runway and strutted down the hall like I was sure my mom had done a million times. And I could have died happy right then with the way my friends clapped and cheered.

I was acting like one of them. I was a diva for real.

We stacked our packages in one chair, then sat in the other four.

"I cannot believe I bought a pair of pants for almost one hundred dollars," Veronique said. "Maybe I should take mine back."

"No!" I said. I really wanted us all to be able to wear the same style for the very first time. "You looked cute in them."

"I don't think my mother's going to think they're too cute. Not when I have to ask for the money I'll need to buy my outfit for the performance because I don't have that much left and I'm not going to be making much more between now and San Francisco."

"Don't worry about it," Diamond said. "We all got your back."

Aaliyah and I nodded.

"But you guys can't always have my back."

"Why can't we?" Aaliyah asked. "You're the one who's always saying we're sisters."

"Not sisters, sistahs," Veronique corrected, then we all laughed.

A guy who didn't look like he was much older than we were came to our table with a pad in his hand. "Hello, ladies. Welcome to the Hamburger Shack. My name is Vick, and I'll be your waiter today." He paused and looked at me. "And how are you beautiful ladies doing?"

I almost fell out of my chair with the way he was staring. He grinned, but I couldn't smile back. I didn't know what had happened to my lips.

"Let's start with you, pretty lady." He was still talking to me. "What're you having today?"

I looked up at him, but only for a second. "I don't want anything."

He frowned a little. "Nothing at all?"

I shook my head.

Diamond said, "Well, I ain't mad at 'cha. Not with the way you're looking." And then she said to the waiter, "She just lost *a lot* of weight."

My mouth and eyes opened wide.

"What?" Diamond asked when she saw my expression. "Honey, you need to be proud of who you are and what you've done. Shoot, you look good, girl." Then she said to the waiter, "But since I'm already cute, I'm gonna have the cheeseburger special with fries and an order of sour cream on the side."

When Veronique and Aaliyah added their own spin to their hamburgers and fries, I kinda squirmed. How was I supposed to do this—sit here, in the middle of this restaurant, with my best friends eating all of my favorite foods?

The guy took our menus and said to me, "Are you sure you won't have anything?"

I shook my head. The moment he stepped away, Diamond said, "He's cute. I think he likes you, India."

Okay, now see—never in my whole life had anyone said a boy liked me.

"Nah," I said.

"Why you're saying nah?" Aaliyah asked. "He was looking at you like you were a piece of cheesecake."

I giggled.

"And why wouldn't he?" Aaliyah continued. "You look good."

Finally! That was the first time my bestest had said anything at all to me about all the weight I'd lost. That was way better than anything that had happened to me—well, almost anything. I don't think there was anything that could top getting into a pair of size ten rhinestone-studded jeans. For that, I'd be willing to starve and throw up for another year.

And then the worst happened.

The waiter brought the food. And put those plates right in front of my nose. I tried not to look at what my friends were eating, but I couldn't help but smell it. I was dying.

Aaliyah said the blessing, then my friends started in on their food. The way my stomach rumbled, I knew it was mad at me.

"You want some of my fries?" Aaliyah asked.

My hand was already moving to her plate before I could even say yes. I just took a couple, but the way those fries tasted—like heaven—I had to have a few more.

While my friends chatted about what they thought the competition would be like in San Francisco, I motioned toward the waiter.

He came over, and grinned when I put in for an order of fries. Then, just before he walked away, I whispered, "Can you add a hamburger to that?"

"Well, I'm glad to see that you're going to eat something," Aaliyah said when my order came.

"Yeah, I wasn't really hungry"—I paused just long enough to take a huge bite of my hamburger—"but I hadn't eaten all day."

Twenty minutes later, I wondered what my friends would think when I ordered another hamburger and more fries. But even though the waiter guy frowned at me, my friends didn't seem to really notice, since they were so busy browsing through a copy of *San Francisco* magazine that Diamond had found somewhere. Now my BFFs were scoping out the best places to shop, to eat, to hang out—they were acting as if they had big money to spend. Only Aaliyah noticed when my second plate came. She frowned, just a little. And I pretended not to see her while Diamond and Veronique kept studying the magazine.

When I finished my second order, I really wanted another hamburger. But I didn't want that waiter to look at me the way he did the last time.

"Ooohhh," Aaliyah said, looking at her watch. "If we don't leave right now, we're gonna be late!"

As she waved her hands in the air for the waiter to bring our check, I grabbed twenty dollars from my purse and tossed it onto the table. "I'm gonna run into the bathroom."

"Hurry up," Diamond said. "We can't be late."

I knew that. But I also knew that I couldn't wait to throw up. Not with everything I'd just eaten. I rushed into the handicap stall, dropped to my knees, and pushed my fingers down my throat. It only took a couple of seconds—I was that good now. But I still hated the way I gagged and the noise I made.

Then I almost jumped out of my skin when I heard that scream behind me.

"India! What are you doing?"

I turned around, and Aaliyah was standing in the stall with me! With a scowl on her face and her hands on her hips.

"What are you doing?" I asked. I thought I had locked the door. "How can you just walk in on me like that?"

"And it's a good thing I did. I knew something was up."

"So you followed me? What are you now? A spy?" I brushed past her like I was way mad. But I was more scared than angry. I didn't know what Aaliyah was going to do. I turned on the faucet full blast at the sink.

"I'm not a spy, but I'm your best friend, remember?" She followed right behind me. "And if you have a problem, then so do I."

"I don't have a problem."

Now she folded her arms and stepped back a little bit. Like she needed to get a better look at me. "You don't have a problem? Then why were you on your knees hugging that nasty toilet?"

Okay, now see—that would have been funny if I *hadn't* been on my knees hugging the toilet. It was going to be kinda hard to convince Aaliyah that I didn't have a problem, so I had to come up with another approach.

"Okay, I was throwing up—"

"Are you out of your mind?"

The way she still screamed, I wondered if I was going to have to try something else.

"No, I'm not," I said as I dried my hands. I rinsed out my mouth, then took a little sip of water. My mouth felt like it was filled with a hundred cotton balls. I guess that was just because I was so scared. I turned back to my bestest. "Aaliyah, this is the first time I've ever done anything like this."

Her eyes became little. And she growled. I guess that was her way of letting me know that she didn't believe me.

"Really, it was the first time I ever did it," I lied. "And I only did it because I've been so good with my diet that I didn't want to mess it up. But I did just mess it up because of the hamburgers I ate." And then I turned it around on her. "That's why I didn't want to come here," I said, hoping she'd remember that coming to the Hamburger Shack was her idea. "I'm trying not to eat hamburgers anymore, but it was so hard to just sit there and watch Diamond and Vee and you eat and eat—"

"That's still no reason."

"I know, and I won't do it again."

"I know you won't because I'm telling. . . ." Aaliyah paused, as if she wasn't sure who to tell. We'd been best friends since forever. It wasn't like we went around telling on each other. "I'm gonna tell Pastor," she said after a moment.

I would have felt better if she'd said she was telling my mom or dad. But why Pastor Ford? That was way, way worse. That was almost like going to God.

"Aaliyah." I tried not to whine, but it was hard. "Please, I said this was my first time. And I'll never do it again."

"But what you're doing is dangerous."

"I know. And it was nasty, too." I made a disgusted kind of face and looked at my hands. "I could never do anything like that again."

Aaliyah stared at me like she could see right through me. "Tell me the truth, is this how you lost all that weight?"

"No!" I said, like her question was the most ridiculous thing I'd ever heard. "How can you lose weight by throwing up?"

I saw it in her face—the way she softened just a little. Like what I said made some sense.

"I lost it all by dieting, Aaliyah. Dieting the right way." And then I said a prayer that Aaliyah would believe my lie and God would forgive it.

"You've got to promise," I started, "not to say anything to anyone. Or else I'll get in big trouble and my mom and dad might even take me out of the Divine Divas. Remember what happened to Diamond when she got in trouble?"

That did it. Of course Aaliyah remembered. Diamond's parents grounded her when they caught her sneaking out with Jax. And her punishment included being pulled out of the Divine Divas. But after about a week, they loosened up and let her back in.

I guess Aaliyah didn't want to take that chance with me. "Okay," she gave in. "But, I swear, India, if I ever see you doing this . . ."

I hugged her. "Don't worry. It'll never happen."

I blew out a big ole breath of air when Aaliyah and I finally walked out of that bathroom.

"What took you guys so long?" Diamond asked. But she was already walking away from us like she wasn't hardly interested in hearing what Aaliyah or I had to say.

Good thing, I thought, as I watched Diamond strut to the door, swinging her shopping bag that held her designer jeans.

Slowly I picked up my bag and looked at Aaliyah. "Thank you," I whispered.

But Aaliyah didn't say a word back to me. Just rolled her eyes and walked away. Like she was way mad. I knew she was, but she was cool. If she said she wasn't going to give me up, then she wouldn't. And by tomorrow, she wouldn't be mad anymore either.

I sighed. This losing weight and keeping secrets added a whole lot of a different kind of weight on me. I wondered if maybe it was time for me to give this whole thing up. I mean, I'd already lost almost thirty pounds. But then I wondered, how could I give it up? Vomiting was all I had to hold onto. It was like my medicine—now I didn't need food all the time to make me feel better. Sometimes, throwing up was enough to make me feel really good.

For the first time in my life, people were looking at me. And if I kept going, in just a little while, I could be wearing a size six or four. Or maybe I could be even better—I could be a size zero. None of my BFFs wore a size zero. And neither did Jill.

I really liked that idea. I would get to a size zero and then I would stop. But until then, all I could do was keep on going and just be way, way more careful.

chapter 19

I didn't break my stride as I sipped my ginger ale. Just kept flipping through the pages like I didn't have to be at school in an hour.

For the first time ever, I saw why Diamond loved these magazines. I used to hate looking at these pictures—all of the skinny girls, all so beautiful, all reminding me of just how ugly I was.

But I didn't feel that way anymore. Not that I was as pretty as any of them. But I had the secret, and soon it might be possible to look almost as good as the models in the magazines.

For a second, I stopped turning the pages. And thought about what had been on my mind for the last couple of days— maybe I should stop before anyone else found out my secret. I mean, Aaliyah busting me on Tuesday was a huge scare. And Sybil and my daddy both still looked at me as if they knew something was up. Seemed like everyone in my world was right there on the verge of finding me out.

Everybody except for Tova. My mom didn't seem to notice—or care about—anything besides me dropping the pounds.

Really, this could be a good time to stop, but the thing was, I was still a size ten.

I glanced down at the magazine and looked at the ad on the page. The advertisement was for tampons, but the girl was so cute and sexy in her skinny jeans and halter top. It was just so much more fun to be thin—even if you were only talking about tampons.

"Honey, what're you doing?" My mom rushed into the kitchen like she had somewhere to go. "You better get moving; I don't want you to be late."

I shook my head and said, "I still have a little time," keeping my eyes on the magazine.

"Did you eat?"

I still didn't bother to look up. "Nope, just this ginger ale."

"You have to eat."

I slowly lifted my head. *My* mother was going to make me eat something? She never cared when I didn't eat—it only seemed to matter to her when I ate.

But she was standing there, right in front of me, staring me down with that look—the same one I was getting from my dad and Sybil and especially Aaliyah. There was nothing but suspicion in her eyes.

When I didn't say anything, my mom added, "You think I'm gonna let you go out of here with only a can of soda for breakfast?" She was already shaking her head. "At least have a bowl of cereal."

Okay, now see—why did my mother want to bust my flow like this? Breakfast was the only meal that was easy for me to skip. But before I could even say anything, she had the box of granola and carton of skim milk sitting on the table in front of me.

"You better get moving," she said and folded her arms like she really meant it.

While Tova stood over me, I spilled granola—just enough to cover the bottom—into the bowl. Then I poured in a little milk. My mother stayed right there until I picked up the spoon.

My dad must've said something, 'cause there was no way Tova would be making me eat. I used to think that if she had her way, I would only eat one day a week.

But she kept standing and staring, and I had to take three more mouthfuls before she finally left me alone.

"I've gotta get going myself. Do you want me to give you a ride to school, or are you too grown for that these days?"

"I'm not too grown, but I like to walk."

My mother's nod felt like a stamp of approval. "That's good exercise." She kissed my forehead. "See you later, honey. Have a great day."

I waited, and when I was sure she wasn't coming back, I jumped up and dumped the rest of my cereal into the garbage disposal. If I wasn't going to throw up anymore, I couldn't afford to eat anything.

I grabbed my backpack and stuffed the magazine inside. But just as I was walking to the door, I thought about the cereal. Right now, all of that was just sitting in my stomach, settling and making me gain weight.

I began to get that feeling that I'd started getting a couple of days ago—like I was going to be way, way sick if I didn't get that food out of me.

Dropping my bag to the floor, I ran into my bathroom, closed the door, pulled the toothbrush out of my pocket, and leaned over the toilet. In less than five minutes, I was up again. There wasn't much to throw up, but I felt better anyway.

I picked up my backpack; my mom was right. I had to get going to school.

chapter 20

The way Diamond hit that last note made my stomach hurt even more.

Even Sybil flinched. "Okay, let's try that one more time. Diamond, we're gonna take it from the top, but you just sing. Ladies"—she pointed to the three of us—"I want to hear you sing and see you step."

I took a deep breath and tried not to think about my stomach hurting or Diamond's singing.

For the last month, since Diamond had become the lead, I'd been worried. Although she could dance something fierce, I think even I could sing better than she could. Her vocals were nowhere near Veronique's, and sometimes she sounded something awful to me.

But since no one else said a word, I wasn't going to be the one to point out that we could be in big trouble now that Diamond had taken Veronique's place.

Since my life was a little better now, I really wanted to win in San Francisco so that we could go to New York. But every time I heard Diamond sing, I began to think that it was gonna take a whole lotta prayers for God to figure out a way to help us win.

But right now, I couldn't think about praying for anyone else but me. Not with the way my stomach was doing its own dance. It took everything I had in me to concentrate so that Sybil would stay all the way off my case. She was always looking especially hard at me, always trying to catch a peek at my fingers.

One of the cell phones rang and we all looked around, because Sybil made it a rule—all phones had to be off. And she wasn't playing.

"Don't worry, ladies." Sybil laughed. "That's mine. I was waiting for a call from Pastor." She flipped the phone open. "Pastor, I'll be right there." Then, back to us, she said, "Take five. I'll be back."

I was the first one to collapse to the floor. That hard wood felt so good; I just wanted to stay right there for the rest of the night. But as good as it felt, it didn't do a thing to stop my stomach from twirling.

"What's wrong with you?" Diamond asked as she handed me a bottle of water.

"I don't know." I took a sip and sighed. That water tasted so good. "I'm not feeling well."

"You don't feel well a lot these days," Diamond said.

"Maybe it's all the weight you lost, my sistah," Veronique added her piece. "Maybe it was too much, too fast."

I didn't even look at Aaliyah. She had made her peace with me, from finding me in the bathroom last week, but I still didn't want to bring all that stuff back up.

I sipped more water, slowly, praying that it would help. I wished I had some ginger ale, but the water tasted good, too. I don't know why I was so thirsty. Seemed like I always was these days.

"Okay, ladies." Sybil came back into the room clapping her hands. "We're going to do this one more time tonight and then we're done."

One more time. I could do it one more time. I pushed myself from the floor but had to stop when I was halfway up. I don't know how I didn't cry, because all I wanted to do was scream with the way my stomach was kicking.

One more time. That's what I kept saying to myself when I finally stood up straight. All I had to do was make it through the song and dance, then I'd be able to go home. And get some ginger ale. And lay down. And then I would feel way better.

"Okay, one, two, three."

Diamond sang and I moved, but the ache felt like it was rising up.

One more time.

Then the ache left my stomach and grabbed my head. My brain started pounding, and at the same time, I started to spin. Round and round. I wanted to tell my friends what was happening, but it was hard to see them through the fog. And my lips were so dry, I couldn't even talk.

"India?"

I turned to the voice, but now I couldn't see anything through the gray air.

"India, are you all right?"

The spinning wouldn't stop, and that made my head hurt even more.

"India?"

That was when the punch came. Hard, to my stomach. And then, to my chest. And another one, to my head.

"Ahhhh!" I screamed. I held my stomach even though my head hurt more.

"India!"

"Ahhhh!" I fell to the ground. It hurt too much to stand up. "Ahhhh!" I just kept screaming.

"India!"

It sounded like everyone was screaming now. But I didn't know. Because I couldn't see. And then, I couldn't hear.

Because everything in my whole wide world became black.

I could hear the voices. Lots of them. But they were so far away. Or maybe it was me—maybe I was the one who was far away. I didn't know anything anymore.

I wanted to open my eyes, but they were shut tight, like someone had put Krazy Glue all over my face. And my mouth, still filled with cotton balls, felt the same way.

But even though I couldn't see and I couldn't talk, I could hear. Everything.

First it was my dad. "Is she going to be all right?" He sounded like he was going to cry.

Next it was my mom. "That's my baby. You've got to do something." She was crying.

And that made me cry, but my eyes were still glued shut.

Still, I cried, "Daddy!" and "Tova!" and then, "Mom, help me."

But before my mom or dad could rescue me, I went to sleep again.

chapter 21

It was like the Krazy Glue was melting away.

Slowly, I pushed my eyes open. And after a moment, I could see. But it was all gray. Everything.

I blinked over and over, until the gray went away and the clear came.

It was clear, but it didn't make sense, because the first thing I saw was the white ceiling. My ceiling wasn't white—it was blue, just like my walls. And all the stuff in my bedroom.

So if I wasn't in my bedroom, where was I? I couldn't have been anywhere in my home, because my mother loved color almost as much as she loved drama. There were no white walls—or ceilings—anywhere in our house.

I tried to push myself up to get a better look, but it was as if the Krazy Glue moved from my eyes to the rest of my body. I felt loaded down, like I was fat again.

"Oh, no," I moaned. I couldn't remember the last time I'd gone to the bathroom. Had I eaten and forgotten to get rid of it?

I had to get up to purge all the food inside of me. But no matter what I did, I felt like I was locked in the bed.

"India? Sweetheart?"

It was just a whisper, but I could tell it was my dad. I had to turn my head all the way to the side to see him. And when he grinned at me, I grinned back. But then I saw my mom right behind him. And there wasn't a smile on her face—she was crying. Not a crying out loud kind of crying—just the sniffling kind.

I'd seen my mother cry before, but only when something way bad had happened. I wondered what could have made her cry this time—had someone died?

Now I wanted to cry, too, even though I didn't yet know who my mother was crying over.

Inside, I prayed, "Please, God, don't let it be one of my aunts or uncles or Grandma Hazel or one of my cousins, especially not Jill."

And then my thoughts got way worse. Suppose it was one of my best friends!

My heart was beating so hard when I asked my mother, "What happened?" I squeezed my eyes shut waiting to hear the answer.

But all my mom did was kiss my forehead, shake her head, and then turn away, still crying.

"What happened?" This time I asked my father.

"You . . . got a little sick, sweetheart." My father took my hand and squeezed it. With his other, he pressed the button that was at the side of my bed. "But you're all right now."

A little sick? I didn't remember that. But whatever was wrong with me had to be way, way bad with the way Tova was crying.

It must've been how I was looking at my mother that made my dad say, "Don't worry, sweetheart. Your mom's fine. She's just glad that you're . . . back with us."

Okay, now see—I was way glad that no one had died, but what my dad just said, that made me want to cry even more. Back with them? What did that mean?

This time, when I looked around the room, it didn't take a minute to figure out that I was in the hospital. It looked like one of those rooms on *Grey's Anatomy*. With the white walls and the blue curtains that hung from the ceiling. And then there was this big ole bed with the silver railing all around it.

But before I could ask my dad what I was doing here, the door swung open and a man who matched the room walked in—from his white, white skin, to the wild mop of silver on top of his head, which I guess was supposed to be his hair, to his white doctor's jacket. He even wore white pants. Only the silver-and-black stethoscope that hung around his neck broke up all of that white.

Okay, so this was a hospital and it didn't take a big brain to figure out this was a doctor.

"Well, I see our patient is awake, huh?" The doctor came over to the other side of the bed. "How are you feeling, India?"

"Fine." I just lay there as he lifted my hand and pressed his fingers against my wrist. I guessed he was taking my pulse. We'd learned how to do that in gym class a couple of years ago.

"Good." Next, he pressed his fingers against my throat, and that made me squirm a bit.

"Does that hurt?" the doctor asked.

"A little. I feel like I have a sore throat." I looked at my mom and dad. Since they weren't saying anything, I guessed it was all right for this doctor to be doing this stuff to me.

Then he took those same fingers and pushed against my stomach. "Ouch!"

But as soon as I screamed out loud like that, I wanted to take it back. Because that made Tova cry even more.

"I'm sorry," the doctor said. "You're still a bit tender there, but that's to be expected."

As the doctor jotted words onto a chart, I wondered when someone was going to tell me what was going on. After a minute or so, he made some kind of motion with his hands, and my mother and father began backing away from the bed.

The doctor rolled a stool closer to me, and my heart started pounding hard again. I don't know why, but I didn't have a good feeling. I kept my head turned all the way to the side so that I could still see my mom and dad. I figured as long as they didn't leave, I would be okay.

Daddy smiled a little, waved a little, and that made it easier for me to breathe.

"India, I'm Doctor Gerard," the man said, getting my attention.

I said, "Hi," although I felt like we'd already been introduced—the way he'd just been poking all over me.

"You're at Cedar Sinai Hospital. Do you remember coming in here?"

I could hardly remember anything—it felt like I'd been sleeping for a long, long time. I pressed my lips together and tried to think back. And then, some of it came to me—the way my stomach had been hurting, then my chest, and my head.

The doctor asked, "Do you remember anything?"

Yeah, now I remembered. "I was at rehearsal," I began. "We were practicing for San Francisco. We were singing and dancing and then . . ." I stopped. I didn't remember anything after that.

"That's right," Dr. Gerard said. "You collapsed. That was yesterday."

Yesterday? "Am I really sick?"

"Well, that's what I want to find out. We had to do a little operation on you."

Operation? Now that was something I definitely didn't remember.

"That's why you're still a little sore," he said, then reached toward my stomach again. But I was not about to let that happen. I tried to scoot to the other side of the bed, but it was hard to move. I was glad when he didn't press his hands against me again. "There are a lot of big words to explain what happened to you, but I'm going to keep this simple. You had a couple of tears—one in your stomach and the other is what we call an upper gastrointestinal tear."

I frowned. That didn't sound simple to me.

"We repaired the tear in your stomach through a very simple operation. The other tear will likely heal on its own."

Wow! I had all of this stuff going on inside of me and didn't even know it.

"India, I need to ask you some questions."

Even though he was talking way over my head, I kind of liked Dr. Gerard. His voice was so soft, so soothing, like he was used to talking to kids.

"We need to figure out how you got those erosions."

I nodded. I kinda wanted to know myself.

"Do you know what happened, India?"

I frowned. I thought I liked this man, but he couldn't have been that good a doctor if he was asking me how I got sick. I hoped my parents hadn't paid him a lot of money.

"India, do you know what happened?" he repeated.

I guess he was going to keep asking me until I answered. "No," I finally said.

"Your mom and dad tell me that you've lost quite a bit of weight recently."

Okay, now see—I didn't want to talk about that. Not with

131

the doctor, because though he didn't seem to know much about stomach stuff, I couldn't take the chance that he might know something about my secret. Maybe I needed to make up something about my secret. Maybe I needed to make up something so that he would keep talking about my stomach.

"Tell me about your weight loss, India," the doctor continued. "How did you do it?"

Just a minute ago, Dr. Gerard sounded good to me. But now he was getting on my nerves. "All I did was go on a diet," I said. "But I want to know what happened to my stomach." I was hoping I had tricked him into changing the subject.

"We'll talk about that," he said. Then he reached for my hands, and by the time I realized what he was doing, it was too late. I had cleaned up my fingernails pretty good, but there were still those marks on my knuckles.

"India," the doctor said as he stood up, "I'm concerned about some other things besides your stomach." He pressed two fingers against my throat. It was gentle, it didn't hurt. "You have enlarged salivary glands."

If my heart wasn't pounding so hard, I would have asked him, what the heck was that?

"And"—now he pressed his fingers against my face—"your cheeks are a bit swollen."

Dang! This doctor was making it sound like I was falling apart. I needed to let him know that I was only fifteen.

"So, India . . ." This time, the doctor didn't sit down. He stood at the railing of my bed and stared down at me. "How did you lose the weight?"

The way Dr. Gerard asked that question, it was almost like he knew. But there was no way I was going to tell on myself—especially not with my mom and dad in the room.

So I lied. "I . . . went on a diet." It wasn't a complete and total lie. The only reason I started throwing up was to lose weight.

Dr. Gerard looked dead in my eyes and shook his head. That was when I knew the gig was up.

"I can't tell you." I kept my voice as low as I could. "I don't want to get in trouble."

"You won't get in trouble," the doctor said.

That's what he thought, but Dr. Gerard didn't know my dad. Sure, my parents weren't all that strict with me, because Daddy always said, "Raise up a child the way they should go, and when they get older, they'll always do the right thing." My dad said he got that straight from the Bible and that since he'd raised me right, he never had to worry.

But every once in a while when I did something wrong, Daddy believed in hard-time punishments. There was no telling what he would do to me if he found out about my secret.

"I'm going to help you," the doctor said as he sat back down on the stool. Rolled it even closer to the bed. "Have you been throwing up?"

I didn't even know I was crying until I felt the tears rolling down my fat cheeks. I nodded.

Over in the corner, my mom started crying again. And this time, it was that real, out-loud stuff. Made me cry harder, too.

The doctor took my hand, then turned to my parents. "I want you all to know that this can be fixed." He looked at me again when he said, "I've discussed this with your parents, India. Are you familiar with the term *bulimia nervosa?*"

Wiping away my tears, I said, "I've heard the bulimia part before."

He nodded. "Well, bulimia nervosa is a psychological eating disorder. But with the proper treatment and counseling and, of course, with your commitment, you'll be fine."

What I really wanted to know was what was Dr. Gerard talking about? Treatment, counseling—he was making it sound like a disease. Like there was something wrong with me. All I'd wanted was to lose weight so that I could stop being the one everyone thought of as the fat girl—if they thought of me at all. I wasn't sick or suffering from some kind of illness.

"The thing is, India," the doctor continued, "bulimia is very serious. The constant throwing up is what caused you to be here. Your stomach suffered some erosion. Parts of your body are extended and swelling because of the trauma you've experienced."

How did a little throwing up do all of that?

And then, Dr. Gerard's voice got stronger, without being loud. "This is very serious, India. Hundreds of girls die each year from complications resulting from bulimia."

"Die?" Oh, my God. I wasn't trying to die. I just wanted to lose weight.

"But I'm confident that with the support of your parents"—he pointed to my mom and dad—"you're going to be all right."

I wanted to look at my parents, but I was too scared. I didn't want to see how disappointed they were in me.

"Oh, baby." My mom came over to me first. "I'm so sorry."

I didn't have a clue in the world what my mother was apologizing for, but my tears were coming so fast, I couldn't even ask her. I wrapped my arms around her and held on tight, just grateful that she still loved me.

Then I felt my dad's teddy bear arms around me. And when I looked up, there were tears coming out of his eyes, too.

Now I felt way, way bad. I'd *never* seen my dad cry, and everybody was crying now—all because of me.

All because I didn't want to be fat anymore.

chapter 22

I felt even worse this morning than I'd felt yesterday. And I'd been feeling this way for at least five minutes.

All I could do was lie in my bed and stare at my mother, slouched over in that little chair. She had slept there all night—because of me.

Last night, when the nurse had come into my room and told my parents that visiting hours were over, I'd been way scared. Even though I'd already been here for one night, I'd been asleep from the surgery. If she left, I'd be awake and by myself.

But before I'd had the chance to say anything, my mother had told the nurse she wasn't going anywhere.

"Ms. Morrow, we'll take good care of your daughter." And then the nurse had looked at me. "You're a big girl, aren't you?"

Yeah, I was a big girl, but what did that have to do with me staying in some big ole hospital by myself? If my mother wanted to stay with me, I didn't see the problem.

The nurse had kept trying to get me to agree with her. "Don't you want your parents to go home to get some rest?"

No! I'd said inside. Why couldn't they have just rested here with me? There was enough room to roll in another bed or two.

But I hadn't had to say a word, because my mother had said, "None of that stuff matters," and she'd waved both hands in the air. "I'm staying."

And that's just what she'd done.

My dad had stayed a little while longer, but after he'd kissed me and my mom good-bye, my mom had climbed right in this little bed and wrapped her arms around me.

At first, the room had been so quiet, it was scary. I'd been sure Tova wanted to know why I'd been throwing up, and I'd really wanted to explain.

But every time I'd opened my mouth, Tova had said, "Hush." She hadn't said it in a mad kind of way, but in a way like she was telling me that everything was okay with her.

So I'd just hugged my mom back because that was my way of saying I was sorry.

Just as I'd been getting sleepy, I'd said, "I love you, Mom."

I'd thought she might get mad, just a little, 'cause Tova really didn't like being called Mom. But when I'd said it, she'd just hugged me even tighter and said, "I love you too, baby." Then she'd held me just like that, until I'd gone to sleep.

I guess that was when my mom got out of the bed and fell asleep in that chair.

"Hey, sweetheart," my dad said as he stepped into the room. When he glanced at my mother, still resting, he lowered his voice. He handed me a bunch of red roses and kissed my cheek.

"Thank you, Daddy."

Then he went over to the side and kissed my mother. She

wiggled a little before she opened her eyes. My father pulled her up and hugged her. And even though they stood there for a long time, I didn't feel as embarrassed as I usually did.

"So did my girls sleep well?" my dad asked.

"I did, but I don't think Tova did."

"I slept just fine," she said. "All I needed was to be here with my baby." My mother kissed me.

"Well, I got you covered now," my dad said before he kissed her. "I want you to go home and get some rest."

She was already shaking her head. "No. I'm staying," she said over and over.

But even though my dad had let my mom stay last night, he wasn't having it today. And in our house, whatever Marvin Morrow said was the law.

Then Pastor Ford came in, and my mom finally agreed to go home.

"But just for a few hours," she said. "And only because you're here, Pastor."

"What about me?" my father kidded. "You don't think I can take care of our daughter?"

We all laughed when my dad made those puppy-dog eyes.

While he walked my mom to the parking lot, Pastor Ford pulled the chair closer to the bed.

"So are you feeling better?" Pastor asked me.

I nodded.

"You gave us quite a scare, you know."

"I'm sorry. I didn't mean to."

"I don't know if Diamond, Veronique, or Aaliyah will ever be the same."

My eyes got way wide. "Are they okay?" I hadn't spoken to any of my best friends, and I wondered if their parents were going to let them come and visit me.

"Oh, they're fine." Pastor Ford waved her hand like she

didn't want me to be concerned about that. "They were all just so worried about you." Her voice got softer when she said, "We all were."

Okay, now see—Pastor Ford was using that voice. That soft one that made me feel bad all over again. Made me feel like I'd let everyone in the whole world down.

Pastor Ford took my hand. "India, why didn't you go to your mom? Or come and talk to me?"

I looked down at my fingers, with the dark edges—the evidence of what I'd done. As I stared at my hands, I paused, taking time to think about Pastor's question. I didn't know what I was supposed to say. What would I have talked to her or my mom about? No one was able to understand.

I shrugged and finally answered, "I don't know what I would have said if I came to you . . . or my mom."

"You could have told us what you were feeling. You can always talk to me about that . . . or anything else."

"It just seemed kind of stupid."

"What?"

"How could I come to you and tell you that I felt bad because I was fat? That sounded stupid."

"Your feelings are always important, never stupid."

"But that's how I felt—fat and stupid."

Pastor looked at me like she was having a hard time believing what I was saying. "India, you're a beautiful girl."

I didn't know if I really believed Pastor Ford. She was just that kind of lady, always saying the right thing. She had to tell me I was beautiful because she was my Pastor and that's probably what God wanted her to say.

"And I'm not just saying that," she said, like she was reading my mind. My best friends and I always kidded about Pastor's Holy Ghost powers. How she seemed to know *everything*. When we were little kids, we all thought God was telling on us

138

to Pastor. I didn't really believe that anymore, but if Pastor had stopped in the middle of a sermon a couple of weeks ago and yelled out to everyone that I'd been throwing up, I wouldn't have been surprised. I'd seen something like that happen so many times.

"India," Pastor continued, "I look at you and see a young lady who is Spirit-filled and beautiful and smart and funny—"

"And fat."

Pastor Ford tilted her head to the side a little. "Why are you defining yourself by your weight?"

Okay, now see—that was a good question, even though I didn't know how to answer. How else was I supposed to define myself? Everyone always defined pretty by your weight. If you were skinny, you were pretty. If you were fat, the best you could hope for was having a pretty face.

Pastor Ford asked, "Don't you know that you're so much more than a number on a scale?"

"I know that. It was just that once we won the gospel talent contest, everybody started calling us stars, and I didn't feel like one. Especially not standing next to Diamond, Veronique, and Aaliyah."

"Did they say that to you?"

"No!" I said so fast that I almost screamed. "They *always* say that I'm fine just the way I am."

"Smart girls. They're right."

"But I wanted to feel and look just like them."

"You think you're not a star?"

"I may be one now, but only because I lost some weight."

Pastor Ford squeezed my hand. "India, before you were born, you were a rising star—to God. And once you accepted Him into your heart, you became His shining star. You've been a star your whole life."

I looked down at my fingers again. "I never felt like one," I whispered.

"That's because you forgot who you belonged to. You're a star for God. It's nice if other people think you are, but none of that lasts. God is the only one who counts. You've got to start seeing yourself the way He sees you."

Pastor Ford's cell phone vibrated, and she read the incoming text. "Oh, I've got to make a call. I'll use one of the pay phones in the hall. You gonna be okay?"

I nodded. It was fine. It was daytime. And I knew that Pastor would be coming back.

Just like my mom and dad had done, Pastor Ford kissed me before she left me alone.

You're a star for God.

I believed Pastor's words. I knew it was important to focus on God first. But I wasn't living in heaven yet. And on earth, I felt more like a star now wearing a size ten than I ever had before.

Even though my secret had been discovered, I just couldn't go back to how it used to be. I would never, ever again be that fat girl with the pretty face.

I didn't know how I was going to do it without throwing up, but I was going to find a way. I still wanted to get down to a size eight, and then a six—and I really got excited when I thought about one day wearing a zero.

Maybe Jill would have some ideas. That whole Hollywood Hills, Beverly Hills crowd always knew what to do. I'd call her as soon as I got home, because San Francisco was in two weeks and I had to be an eight by then.

I was going to do what Pastor said. I was going to remember that I was a star for God. But at the same time, I was going to look like a star for the rest of the world, too.

chapter 23

I had to get out of this hospital!

This was the second night that my mom had slept in that chair. It had to be horrible for her. And not only that, right now she was in the bathroom brushing her teeth and washing up. Tova Morrow, Drama Mama, did not live like that.

But what was way, way worse was that they were making me eat all of this food. And with someone always being around, there was no way I could throw up, even though that was what I really wanted to do.

This whole thing was getting scary. All I could think about was San Francisco and how much weight I still needed to lose.

I pushed the food tray from in front of me and glanced around the room for a hiding place—somewhere I could dump this bowl of cereal while my mother was still in the bathroom. Then I saw the vase full of the roses my dad had given me. *That's it,* I thought. The water might end up looking kind of funny, but that wasn't my problem.

Slowly, I dropped my feet to the floor and picked up the bowl. But just as I stood up, Tova swooped into the room.

"Did you finish eating?" she asked.

She was unbelievable. My mother hadn't slept for more than a few hours in the last couple of days, and when she had slept, she'd been hunched over the side of some hard hospital chair. Still, she looked scrubbed-clean, fresh-faced, model-perfect.

My mom's eyes went straight to the bowl in my hand, and she frowned. "Doesn't look like you've eaten a thing."

"I wasn't all that hungry," I said, and before she could protest, I added, "I think it was because of that big dinner I had last night."

She put her hands on her hips. "You call a chicken leg, a tablespoon of rice, and carrots a big dinner?" She pushed the tray back in front of me. "You'd better eat this." She was smiling, but she wasn't playing with me.

So I did what she said. But I hated every spoonful. All of this food was just settling in my stomach—with no way for me to get rid of it.

I had to bust out of this place—and soon.

I was halfway through with this doggone cereal when the door to my room swung open again. "Good morning, India." It was Dr. Gerard, and a little Asian lady followed behind him. I almost kissed the doctor. At least now I wouldn't have to finish my breakfast.

The Asian woman shook hands with my mother as if they'd met before. And then they all turned to me.

"India, I have some good news." Dr. Gerard spoke first. "We're releasing you today."

I clapped my hands, feeling like I was being set free.

Dr. Gerard smiled. "I know you're ready to go home. We just wanted to make sure that you were healing."

"I feel fine, Dr. Gerard." I really did. It still was a little sore around my stomach area, but I knew once I got up and back with my friends, I'd be all the way fine.

"India," he said and then stepped aside, "this is Dr. Yee. She's going to be working with you."

"It's nice to meet you, India." She shook my hand.

Dr. Gerard said, "India, I've been helping you heal physically, and Dr. Yee is going to be working with you"—he turned to my mother—"and your parents to heal psychologically."

I frowned. Okay, now see—this had started out all right, but I had a bad feeling about this psychological stuff.

"Are you a psychiatrist?" I asked.

Dr. Yee smiled, and her lips almost took up her whole face. "I'm a psychotherapist."

Okay, so what was that? But no matter what she was, I didn't need someone like Dr. Yee. It wasn't like I was sick or anything. If I wanted to stop throwing up, I would stop doing it. I just didn't want to. Not until I got to a size zero.

"In the beginning," Dr. Yee continued, "I'm going to be working with you three days a week after school."

I frowned. I didn't know how she was going to do that. Since San Francisco was just two weeks away, there was no way I could miss any practices.

I looked at my mom before I said, "Dr. Gerard, I don't think I need another doctor. I know what I did was wrong, and I won't do it again."

"It's good that you feel that way," Dr. Yee answered even though I wasn't talking to her. "But it will be much better if you understand some of the reasons why you started purging." She smiled. "And I'm just going to help you figure all of that out."

Inside, I screamed, *I was fat! That's why I did it.*

Outside, I had to be polite. "Dr. Yee, I really don't need any help, and even if I did, I wouldn't be able to do that now. After school, I have practice . . ."

Both of the doctors frowned, but only Dr. Yee said, "Practice?"

I nodded. "For the Divine Divas. It's a singing group that I belong to. And we're competing in San Francisco. And I already missed two practices this week. And—"

Dr. Gerard held up his hand. He looked at my mother, then turned back to me. "India, you won't be competing with the Divine Divas."

I threw all that polite stuff out the window. "What are you talking about?" He wasn't making any sense, and how could he? He didn't know a thing about the Divine Divas. But instead of Dr. Gerard answering, my mother came over to the bed.

"Honey," she started softly, "you won't be competing with the girls this time around."

"No, Tova. Why?" I cried.

"You just had surgery, and it would be too much."

"But I feel fine."

Dr. Gerard put in his two cents. "Your body needs time to heal."

Okay, I needed to say that louder or something, 'cause these adults weren't hearing me. So I repeated, "I feel fine."

My mother said, "I know you do, and we want to keep it that way."

"But I have to go to San Francisco. I *have* to be on the stage. If not, they'll kick the Divine Divas out of the competition." Maybe my mother didn't remember the rules, but I did. How you started was how you had to finish—meaning that the same people who were singing in the first contest had to compete in San Francisco and New York and Miami. You couldn't have a change of talent. That's why the contest director had told all the churches to choose their groups carefully.

So if I couldn't perform, then the Divine Divas would be history. There was no way I was going to let my friends down.

"Tova," I said, this time a little louder, "I have to go to San Francisco." I crossed my arms like that would mean something. "And that's final." I'd never, ever spoken to my mother like that, but I didn't care. None of these people were getting it—none of them were understanding how important the Divine Divas were to me and my BFFs. "I'm going to San Francisco!" I yelled.

"Whoa, what's going on in here?"

When my dad walked into the room, I had some hope. He always told me about all the great things he'd learned as a football player. Like how important teamwork and commitment was. He would understand that I couldn't let down my friends.

"Daddy," I cried. "They won't let me go to San Francisco and compete with the Divine Divas!"

And then it felt like my heart just stopped beating. It was the way my father looked at me—all sad—like he'd known about this the whole time. And what was way, way, way, way worse was that I could tell he agreed with everyone but me.

My daddy looked at me, and his eyes said he was sorry before his mouth did. But he did say, "I'm sorry, sweetheart." He said it real soft, as if the whisper would help his words not hurt so much. But even before he said it, I could have told him that his words did hurt—a lot.

"I'm sorry, but you can't compete." He kissed the top of my head, as if that was going to help. "You just can't, sweetheart."

I was already crying by the time my father put his arms around me. In front of Dr. Gerard and Dr. Yee, in front of my mom and dad, I cried like a big ole baby.

I cried because I knew no matter what I said, my father's word was the law.

chapter 24

I cried all the way home.

And I didn't say a word to my parents. I planned to never, ever speak to them again.

How could they do this to me? They were ruining my whole life, but not only mine—Diamond's, Veronique's, and Aaliyah's, too. I tried to explain it to them, but they didn't even care.

So if they didn't care about me, I didn't care about Marvin or Tova either!

"It's time to get out."

I was so mad, I didn't even notice that my dad had stopped and we were already in front of our house. I'd been away for three days, and this morning I'd been so excited to be coming home. But not now. I didn't have anything to look forward to except school and afternoons filled with some psychotherapist I didn't even need.

"Are you all right, honey?"

I looked at my mother, and the only reason I didn't roll my

147

eyes was because my mother didn't play that. I just turned around without saying a word to her.

As soon as I did that, my father said, "India, did you hear your mother?"

Since my father *definitely* didn't play that, I said, "Yes."

"Then answer her."

I turned around as slowly as I could and glared at my mother. "I'm. Fine."

Why was she asking me if I was all right, anyway? It wasn't like she cared. I was way madder at my mother than my father because I had always been able to count on her to be on my side whenever it came to any kind of special projects I wanted to do. When I first told her about Diamond's idea to form this group, she was as excited about the Divine Divas as I was. That's why I couldn't figure out why she was dropping me like that now. Didn't she know how hard I had worked? It was because of all of my hard work that I'd ended up in the hospital in the first place. And now it was all being taken from me because my mother and father wanted to ruin my life.

I marched to the front door but stopped because I didn't have my keys. All I wanted to do was get into the house and go into my bedroom forever. I hoped Marvin and Tova weren't going to make me eat dinner with them. I didn't want to do anything with them ever again. If I was eighteen years old, I would have just moved out of the house.

As my dad was putting the key in the door, he said, "So, do you have any plans for this afternoon?"

What kind of question was that? I couldn't have any plans. I just got out of the hospital. And my best friends were still in school—not that I was all that excited about seeing them. How was I going to tell them what my parents were doing to us?

Aaliyah would be a little sad, but she'd be all right. But

Diamond and Veronique—they were way into this star thing and would probably never speak to me again.

"No, I don't have any plans." I only answered my father because I didn't want him on my case.

I might have had to talk to my parents, but I didn't have to look at them. I didn't look up at my mother or father as they walked into the house in front of me. I didn't look up when I stepped inside and dropped my bag in the foyer.

I didn't look up until I heard, "Surprise!"

I almost jumped out of my skin. "Oh, my God!" I said, so shocked. But I was way, way happy when I looked at the living room filled with balloons and streamers—and my best friends.

"What are you doing here?"

They rushed, then tackled me so hard, I fell against the wall.

"What do you think we're doing here?" Aaliyah asked, still hugging me.

"Yeah, my sistah, did you think we'd let you come home without us?"

"We're your best friends in the whole world," Diamond added. "Of course we'd be here. And it helped that your mom got permission for us to miss our afternoon classes today. Hey!" She held her hands in the air and did a little dance.

If Diamond wasn't being so silly, I would have cried. I couldn't believe what my BFFs had done, as I looked up at the sign in front of the window that said WELCOME HOME, INDIA!

They'd done all of this, and now I was going to have to ruin their lives.

"Come in here," Diamond said as she grabbed my hand, "and tell us all about it."

I followed my friends. "Well, it's not like some great story."

"Are you kidding?" Diamond said, all dramatic. "Remember

149

when my brother broke his leg skiing a couple of years ago? Well, that was good enough to get him a new car. You're gonna get something out of this."

It wasn't until I heard my father laugh that I remembered my parents were even here. And when I looked up at them, all the good feelings I had from my friends went away.

"I don't think India's going to get a car, Diamond." My father was still laughing. "But we might have a couple of surprises for her." To me, he said, "Catch up with your friends, but make sure you don't overdo it, okay?"

"We'll take care of her, Mr. Morrow," Aaliyah said.

I didn't say anything and was glad when he and Tova finally left me alone with my friends.

I must've had a pitiful look on my face, because Aaliyah asked, "What's wrong with you?"

I couldn't even get a word out before Diamond said, "You're supposed to be the smart one. What do you think is wrong with her? She just got out of the hospital." Diamond shook her head like she couldn't believe Aaliyah hadn't figured that out.

But Aaliyah wasn't fazed by Diamond; she stared as if she knew for sure there was something else going on with me. Like always, I couldn't hide a single thing from my bestest—which meant I had to break it down for my friends right now.

"I have some bad news."

Diamond fell back onto the couch. "What?" she said in a voice that sounded like she was about to faint. "Please don't tell me that the doctors found something really wrong with you and that you're really, really sick. I couldn't take it!"

If I wasn't so sad, I would have cracked up at my friend. Straight drama!

Veronique rolled her eyes at Diamond, but Aaliyah hadn't taken her eyes away from me.

"What is it?" Aaliyah asked.

I had to take a deep breath. "I'm not going to be able to sing with y'all in San Francisco."

None of my friends moved.

"And . . . ," Veronique said.

"And?" It was totally clear that they hadn't heard me. "I said, I'm not going to be able to compete, and that means that you may not be able to compete either."

"So, what's the new part, because we already knew that," Aaliyah said.

I blinked a couple of times just to make sure that I was awake and hearing right.

Diamond said, "Yeah, Pastor Ford and Sybil talked to us on Wednesday."

Aaliyah picked up the story. "They told us what had happened to you, and how this would affect the Divine Divas."

Veronique asked, "So, what's the big thing you had to tell us?"

I looked at my friends. "You guys aren't upset?"

"Well, we were upset at first," Diamond said, "because when we heard you were having an operation it scared us."

"But once we found out that you were all right," Aaliyah added, "then we were all right, too."

"But what about San Francisco? What about the Divine Divas?"

They all shrugged and Aaliyah said, "Pastor Ford is working on it. She's calling everyone she knows to explain the situation."

"And if there is anyone who can make this happen, my sistah, it's Pastor."

The tears that I had wanted to hold back didn't stay away now. I had the best friends in the whole world. "I was worried that you guys were going to be mad at me."

Diamond said, "Well, I *was* mad at you, a little, at first." She bit the corner of her lip like she didn't want to say the rest to me. "Why did you do it, India? Why were you throwing up?"

I looked at Aaliyah. "Did you tell them?"

She shook her head. "I told you I wasn't going to give you up, but now I wish I had."

"Hold up." Veronique stuck her hand in the air. "Are you telling me that you knew all about this?"

I spoke before Aaliyah could say a word. "She didn't know anything," I said. "Just one time, she found me . . . but she didn't really know."

"I still feel like I could've done something," Aaliyah said.

"There's nothing you could have done, because I wanted to throw up."

Diamond scrunched her face. "That sounds so nasty."

"Trust, it is."

"So why, my sistah?"

All of my friends were looking at me with wide eyes, as if they were about to hear a horror story. I guess for them, throwing up would be horrible because fat wasn't a part of their lives. I didn't think they would ever be able to understand, but I still said, "I was tired of being the fat girl."

"You were never fat," Aaliyah said.

Diamond said, "She's right, and I hope you're going to stop doing that throwing up stuff because the judge said that purging could kill you."

Veronique and Aaliyah nodded their agreement.

"Yeah, I'm gonna stop," I said, hoping that was the truth. But I just didn't know. Even now, I felt like I had to throw up, and I hadn't even eaten anything since breakfast. "I'm going to be working with a doctor who's supposed to help me, but all I can think about is how I messed it up for the Divine Divas."

"Don't worry about that, my sistah. You didn't mess up a

thing. My mom told me that your purging wasn't all your fault. Sometimes there's something that happens in the brain."

"Yeah, my dad told me something like that, too," Aaliyah said.

I didn't know about that—but what I knew was that my friends were the bomb!

"So don't worry about San Francisco," Diamond said.

"We're fine about it," Aaliyah said.

"And I have a good feeling. Whatever is supposed to happen, will happen," Veronique said. Then she reached out her arms and hugged me again. And Diamond and Aaliyah joined in the group hug.

"All you have to think about now is that we're sisters," Diamond said.

"Yeah," the other two piped in.

But I didn't say a thing. Just closed my eyes and hugged my friends tight. And said a little prayer to God thanking Him for giving me the best sisters in the whole wide world.

chapter 25

I had been really mad at my parents, but as soon as Diamond, Veronique, and Aaliyah left my house yesterday, I got over it. I mean, if my parents would go to all the trouble of having my best friends meet me at home, and letting us have a little party in the afternoon, then I guess they weren't so bad.

But things were still really weird. First, last night, I found out that I wouldn't be going back to school yet.

"I'm not going to school all next week?" I asked when my father told me.

"No, the doctors think it's best that you stay home for a week."

"But I feel fine," I said, thinking about what I was going to do in the house for a whole week. Talk about boring.

"We know you're fine, honey," my mom said. "But it's more than that. We want to make sure that you're fine all the way."

Okay, now see—I knew that was code for We have to make

sure that you won't start purging again. But how were they going to stop that? Even if I didn't go to school, they couldn't watch me every minute of the day.

At least that's what I thought. But my mother and father ended up doing a pretty good job of making me feel like I was in prison. First, after Diamond, Veronique, and Aaliyah left, my mother sat in my bedroom with me, as if she was making sure that I didn't throw up the cake I'd shared with my friends.

After dinner, she and my dad did the same thing—they watched me like a hawk, and even when I went to the bathroom, I didn't do anything, 'cause I knew they were right outside, probably listening at the door the same way I listened to them in their bedroom.

Then, when I told my parents good night, my dad hugged me and said, "By the way, India, keep your bedroom door open."

I couldn't believe they were playing me this tight. When I got in my bed, I didn't make any moves, because I was sure if I did, some kind of alarm would've gone off and a voice would've started yelling, "Danger, danger, danger!" all through the house.

Even now my mother was sitting in my bedroom as I took my shower.

Ever since Dr. Gerard introduced me to Dr. Yee, I had been freakin' out that I had to see some psycho-doctor. But now I was thinking maybe she'd be able to help me out! Maybe after our session, my parents would cut me a little slack.

At ten minutes to ten, my dad let my mother and me out of the car in front of a building right next to the Santa Monica pier. And by the time he parked the car and met us inside, Dr. Yee was ready for us.

"I'm so glad to see you this morning, India." Dr. Yee was sitting behind this big ole desk that seemed way too big for her. "How've you been feeling?"

"You mean since you saw me yesterday?" Okay, so I was being a little sarcastic. But this psycho stuff was creepy. I mean, it wasn't like I was crazy or anything, so why did I have to see this doctor?

But with the way my father glared at me, I knew that was going to be the last smart-mouthed thing I would say to Dr. Yee or anyone—at least for today.

Although my dad didn't like what I'd said, Dr. Yee didn't seem to mind. She just smiled and said, "India, I wanted to do this first session on the weekend because it's important that we get started right away."

She must've thought that I needed a lot of help if she couldn't even wait until Monday to see me.

She said, "These sessions are all about you. Anytime you have a question, or you want to say anything, just jump in, okay?"

I shrugged a little, nodded a lot. All I wanted to do was get this over with.

"But there is one thing I'm going to ask you, India. I need you to be completely honest about everything. Do you think you can do that?"

I nodded.

"No matter what we talk about, the only way it will work is if you say what's really on your mind and what's really in your heart, okay?"

It seemed like she was asking me the same question over and over, but I nodded anyway.

"Okay." Dr. Yee leaned forward. She wasn't smiling anymore. It looked like she was about to get real serious. She said, "Tell me about yourself, India."

Okay, now see—that kinda surprised me. I thought she was

gonna jump right on my case, asking me how long I'd been throwing up and why I was doing it and all kinda stuff like that.

That's what I really wanted—I wanted Dr. Yee to ask me why. Then I was gonna ask her if she knew what it was like to be fat. Dr. Yee didn't even look like she weighed one hundred pounds. She couldn't possibly know anything about what I'd been through—which made it even more stupid that I was sitting here talking to the psycho-doctor.

But since my dad was sitting right next to me, all I said was, "What do you want to know about me?"

"Tell me about school. What grade you're in, what subjects you like . . ."

Boring!

"Who are your friends?"

Now that was a question I could get with. I said, "I have three best friends."

Dr. Yee smiled. "Three? Most people don't even get to say they have one. You're really blessed."

I always thought I was blessed—at least until yesterday, when my mom and dad took the Divine Divas away from me.

"Yeah, Diamond, Veronique, and Aaliyah have been my best friends since we were little. And then a couple of months ago, we formed a singing group to compete. But now *nobody* will let me be in the contest."

I waited for my mother to say something, or definitely my father. But they just sat there, my father in between me and my mother, like everything I was saying was okay.

"How does that make you feel—that you're going to miss the singing competition?"

How do you think? was what my head said. But I was smart enough not to say that out loud.

So what I said was, "I feel really bad about it. I've *ruined* my best friends' lives. We were gonna win that competition and get a contract, but now we won't even get to go to San Francisco, and it's all because of me."

"Besides what's happened with the Divine Divas, do you think a lot of bad things happen because of you?"

"Sometimes, but this is *definitely* my fault."

"So, explain this to me—how it's your fault. What happened?"

Okay, I was trying to figure out what the psycho-doctor was up to, because she already knew exactly what had happened. I said, "We can't go to San Francisco because I got a little sick."

"Sick?"

I didn't really feel like going through the whole thing—especially with my parents sitting right there.

"How did you get sick, India?" the doctor asked.

She wasn't going to let this go, so I pretended that my parents weren't sitting right next to me. "Dr. Gerard said it was because of purging, but I don't see how—"

Dr. Yee didn't even let me finish. "It was definitely because of the purging. So, let's talk about that."

I sucked in a deep breath.

"Do you know what purging is, India?"

Okay, now see—that was a stupid question. "Yeah, purging is throwing up."

"That's what you *do* when you purge, but that's not what it is. Purging is a psychological eating disorder."

I knew that already—from Dr. Gerard.

"That means it has more to do with your mind than it does with your body. Eating disorders rarely have anything to do with food and weight alone."

I really didn't have any kind of idea what Dr. Yee was talking about, but I could tell her what purging meant to me. Purging took away a lot of my worries—I didn't have to worry about being really fat anymore. Or being invisible. Or people making fun of me. Or talking about me. Or not liking me.

"India, why do you think you started purging?"

I was ready for that question. "Because I was fat."

"How did being fat make you feel?"

Now, this question, I didn't expect. I didn't even know what to say, because no one had ever asked me that before. I tried to think about when all of this started, when I was really fat. And all of those bad feelings came back to me. "I felt like I didn't fit in with Diamond and Vee and Aaliyah."

"But aren't they your best friends?"

"They are," my voice was softer now, "but they're skinny, and pretty, and smart."

"And you don't think you are?"

I don't know why she asked me that. All she had to do was look at me and she would know the answer. "I'm none of that."

"But you've lost weight. Hasn't that changed anything for you?"

"I mean, I look a little better, but I still don't look as good as my friends."

"What do your friends think of you?"

"They like me. We're like sisters."

"Did they like you when you were heavier?"

"Yeah, but my friends don't really look at me. They kinda just forget about the outside and just look at me on the inside. That's why they really like me, I think. But nobody else does that. Everyone else only sees my outside. And if they don't like the outside, then they don't like me."

Dr. Yee stopped with all the questions for just a moment, and I took a big breath.

"That's a very good explanation, India." Dr. Yee looked like she was a little sad. "So, your friends were the only ones who looked inside of you."

I gave her a big-time nod.

Then she hit me with a shocker. "What about your parents?"

Okay, now see—Dr. Yee had me going so much, I kinda forgot that my parents were even in the room. How was I supposed to answer that with my mom and dad sitting right there?

"India, remember I asked you to be completely honest?"

"Uh-huh."

"Would you feel better talking to me alone?" Dr. Yee asked.

Before I could answer, my mom leaned forward so that I could see her whole face. "Honey, we're going to do this whichever way you want, but I really wish that you'd talk to Dr. Yee with me and your dad here."

I still didn't look at her straight, but I kinda took a peek. Her eyes were watery, like she was about to cry. I didn't know if it was because of anything I'd said or if she was just sad because she didn't want to leave the room.

My mother said, "I really want to stay, India. I want to hear all the ways that your dad and I can help you get better. So, please, talk to us." She took a deep breath and added, "Even if you think what you have to say will hurt."

From the corner of my eye I could see my dad nodding, but this still didn't seem cool to me. "I don't want to get in trouble."

"You won't, sweetheart," my daddy said. "You're telling us how you feel. No one should ever get in trouble for that."

Okay, I just hoped that he'd remember that. And I hoped he'd remember that Dr. Yee told me to tell the whole truth.

When I looked at Dr. Yee, she went right back to business.

"So what about your parents, India? Do you think they see the inside or the outside of you?"

This time, I sucked in a big ole gasp of air, but my voice still came out kinda soft. "My dad doesn't look at the outside of me. Only the inside. I think that's why he likes me." I stopped for a second. "But my mom"—I did everything I could to keep my eyes on the doctor—"she only looks at the outside. And that's why I think she never liked me."

"India!" my mom cried.

"I think that's why she never wanted me to call her Mom," I said before I could help it. "I think she didn't want to look at me and see someone so fat and ugly calling her Mom."

I heard my mother take a deep breath, and then I felt bad. But they had all told me to be honest.

Dr. Yee said, "So you don't think your mother loves you?"

"I think she loves me because she has to since I'm her daughter. I just want her to like me, too."

"I do like you, honey," my mother said, reaching for me across my father's lap. "I can't believe you don't know that."

When I looked at my mother, there were tears in my eyes, too. "I don't think you really, really like me. I think you're beginning to like me better because I lost weight. And I think if I can make it to a size zero, you'll like me the way Daddy does."

My mother put her hand over her mouth and started sobbing like she was a baby. And now I felt way, way bad.

"I'm sorry," I said to her.

She shook her head as my father gave her a tissue. "This is all my fault," she sobbed.

Dr. Yee held up her hand. "Mrs. Morrow, there are no faults here—only solutions. You know that you love India. We just have to find a way for India to stop equating love with weight."

My mom and my dad both nodded, and then my dad took

my hand. With his other one, he held my mother. When she stopped crying, I felt a little bit better.

Dr. Yee said, "I think we've accomplished a lot this morning."

Thank goodness, I thought to myself. It sounded like Dr. Yee was going to let us go; this would be over—at least for today.

"I do have one last question for you, India."

Uh-oh. The way she said that, I had a feeling this wasn't going to be good.

The doctor said, "Once again, you can be honest. There's no way to get in trouble here."

I'm not sure I all-the-way believed that, but after what I'd said about my mother, I guess there was no reason not to tell the truth about anything else.

"Are you still purging?"

I took a breath and shook my head. "I haven't, but . . ." I stopped and wondered if I was supposed to be totally honest. "I've thought about it . . . a lot."

I heard my mother take in another deep breath.

"But I haven't done it," I repeated, just so everyone would get it straight.

"That's good," Dr. Yee said, "because it's really dangerous, as you found out." She leaned forward on her desk like she really wanted me to hear what she had to say next. "Every year, so many girls die from complications caused by purging. . . ."

I knew that. I had been thinking about that ever since Dr. Gerard had told me.

"So, what we're going to do, India, is help you reach all of your objectives in a healthy way." Then she turned to my parents. "I'm not going to prescribe any medication. I don't think that's necessary."

As the doctor kept talking, my father stood up and walked closer to her desk. He answered some questions and my mother just sat, looking all sad—which is exactly the way I felt. I didn't want my mother to feel bad about anything I'd said. She was a great mom to me. I just wasn't sure if I was a good daughter for her.

Slowly, I moved my hand and reached for my mother. She turned, looked at me, then took my hand. She held me tight, until she finally smiled.

chapter 26

All day long everybody had been so nice to me.

In the cafeteria, the kids who sat at our table talked to me as if they hadn't been ignoring me for the two years I'd been at Holy Cross Prep. And then the teachers were way cool, too. Mr. Berg and Mrs. Watson told me that if I needed extra time on my projects, I could have it. And my gym teacher, Ms. Jaffe, told me to take it easy for a few days, which was all right with me.

I wasn't sure if everyone liked me now because I'd been sick or because I'd lost so much weight. But whatever it was, it was working for me.

Things at home were working, too. Although my parents were still playing me tight, it was getting better. I hadn't purged since I'd gone into the hospital almost two weeks ago. But even though I hadn't thrown up, I was still thinking about it . . . all the time. Especially when I looked down at the food on my plate every day—all I wanted to do was go straight to the bathroom and get rid of it. I didn't, though, because after everybody kept telling me about kids dying from purging, I wasn't trying to be one of those statistics. It was hard, but so far, I'd been able to play it straight.

But the best part of being back at school was hanging with my BFFs. They'd been on me all day—especially Aaliyah. Even though we only had homeroom together, she was waiting for me in the hallway at the end of every period. I don't think anyone had asked her to keep an eye on me—but you know Aaliyah. She had this parental thing going on.

Like just now, she made this big announcement that she was going to walk me home.

"What's up with that?" I slammed my locker shut. Even though this had been a good day, I was glad that it was finally over. I was way tired—I guess being off from school for almost two weeks would do that to you. "Why would you want to walk me all the way home?"

Aaliyah shrugged. "I just want to hang out a little longer."

"Do you want us to all walk you home?" Diamond asked.

Before I could answer, Veronique whined, "I can't. I've got to get home because D'Andre's sick and my grandmother has to go somewhere."

"That's okay," I said. "You guys don't have to babysit me. I keep telling everybody that I'm fine."

Diamond shrugged. "Okay. Anyway, we'll hang big soon for sure. We'll all go out and celebrate your being back at school."

But the way Aaliyah looked at me, I knew she was not backing down. I had a feeling that Aaliyah just wanted to make sure that I wasn't going to make a pit stop—and grab a couple of hamburgers and apple pies—on my way home. I wasn't planning to do that, but honestly, I couldn't say that I wouldn't. I mean, walking by those golden arches—I didn't know if I was going to be tempted or not. So maybe it was a good thing that Aaliyah wanted to act like my bodyguard.

Last week in one of our sessions, Dr. Yee warned me that temptation was coming. Not only to purge, but to binge, too. I didn't have to worry about my stash anymore because I got rid of that box for good, but there were still all kinds of temptations in front of me—in the stores I passed on my way to school, in the cafeteria, with the kids in class who always had snacks—all over the place.

But Dr. Yee was teaching me all kinds of ways to handle it. Like the way she was trying to get me to think about food. She told me to try not to think about the food settling and building up in my stomach. Instead, she said, to think of it as friends because when eaten right, food could actually help me. And then she told me that eating certain foods like bananas and apples and oatmeal would burn fat—now, I could get with that.

Dr. Yee also had this crazy exercise she wanted me to do. She actually asked me to look at myself naked in the mirror. At first, I thought that was so gross! Why would anyone want to do that? But then Dr. Yee explained that I should never look at my body as gross—and that it was a process and one day I'd be able to stare in the mirror and see how beautiful I was.

Yeah, right!

She wanted me to look at my naked body for five minutes every day.

An even bigger yeah, right!

But I was doing it—at least a little. Every morning when I got out of the shower, I took a peek in the mirror. I wasn't primpin' and posin' like the doctor wanted—I would only look for like two or three seconds. But that was way more than I'd ever done before. At the rate I was going, in ten years I'd be able to do the five-minute thing.

What Dr. Yee didn't know was that I was still weighing myself. She told me to stay away from the scale and just look at the way my clothes were fitting. But I needed that scale to make sure I wasn't gaining any weight. Those numbers were what kept me going to at least try to get this bulimia thing all the way right.

Dr. Yee had told me that doing it right wasn't going to be easy, and that's why I wasn't really trying to talk Aaliyah out of walking me home. Plus, it was gonna be fun to hang with my bestest for a little while longer, since I'd missed all of them so much.

"Okay," I finally gave in to Aaliyah. "You can walk me home."

She raised her eyebrows. "Like I need your permission. You must've forgotten who I am."

We all laughed.

But while they kept laughing, I stopped. And looked at my friends, all happy now. I wondered if they'd heard anything. I'd wanted to ask them all day, and now I couldn't put it off anymore. I took a deep breath. "Any news from Pastor yet?"

The way the three of them stopped laughing and looked at each other before they turned to me made my heart start pounding hard. They *had* heard something. And from the look on Diamond's face especially, it couldn't be anything but bad news.

I wanted to cry right there. I had ruined everybody's lives, and because of me, my friends would never be stars. I was lucky they were still speaking to me.

I was scared to ask, but I had to know. "So, what did Pastor say?"

Veronique and Aaliyah looked at Diamond, and she said, "Well, it's not the best of news."

"I'm so sorry," I said before she could get the last word out. I didn't want to stand in the school hallway and cry, but I could feel the tears coming.

And just as I was about to open my mouth and bawl like a

big ole baby, my best friends yelled, "Sike!" And then they were bending over laughing, cracking up, while I was standing there looking stupid.

"What I meant to say," Diamond was still giggling as she tried to talk, "was that it's not the best of news for the competition, 'cause we're going to San Fran and we're gonna smoke it!" She took my hand. "We're going to San Fran, Indy. Pastor explained it all to Glory 2 God, and the only exceptions that can be made for changes in a group are medical emergencies. So we're still in it to win it!"

"Oh my God!" I put my hands over my mouth to stop from crying and screaming and being all happy right there in the hallway. "You're still going to San Francisco!"

"Yeah!"

I hugged all my best friends, so excited for them. But there was a big part of me that was way sad. I wouldn't be going. And after they won in San Francisco, would they even want me back in the group?

Then Diamond said, "And when we win this, then we'll be on our way to New York and you'll be back with the Divine Divas," as if she had heard everything I was thinking.

"She won't be back," Veronique piped in and turned to me. "You're still a Divine Diva, my sistah. You're just on a little leave of absence."

I nodded. "I'm so happy for you guys."

"Be happy for yourself, too," Diamond said. "I expect you back singing and dancing as soon as we get back from San Fran this weekend," she said, like she was the one in charge.

"I gotta get going," Veronique said.

"Me, too," Diamond added before they both hugged me.

As Aaliyah and I walked to the other end of the building, she said, "You should come to the rest of our practices this week."

"Okay," I said, putting a smile on my face, but I knew there was no way I would. I had the sessions with Dr. Yee, and my parents weren't about to let me miss any of those. And anyway, although I was really happy for my best friends, it would just make me way, way sad to watch them singing and dancing, since I wasn't going to be anywhere near San Francisco.

But I took a deep breath and tried to push it out of my mind. There was no use thinking about it—it was never going to happen.

I guess all I needed to do now was concentrate on not purging and on praying for my sisters, that they would bring it and win it in San Francisco.

My legs were crossed, yoga-style, while I sat on my bed staring at my jewelry box. I was supposed to be picking out the pieces that I wanted to give to Diamond, Veronique, and Aaliyah so they could wear them in San Francisco. But I hadn't picked out a thing because I couldn't stop thinking about how I wasn't going. And how no one would miss me.

I felt bad all over again.

Just when my life had been going good, I had to go mess it up and get sick. Now I was going to be invisible for real.

But I guess it didn't matter how much I thought about this or moped about it, because nothing was going to change. No matter how I looked or how I felt, I wasn't going. All because of that stupid purging thing.

It was good that I didn't have my stash in my closet, 'cause right about now, I could use a piece of cake. And if I started eating, I might never stop.

Dumb! Dumb! Dumb! was what I was thinking when my mom stuck her head into my bedroom.

"Hey, what 'cha doin'?"

"Nothin'."

Sitting across from me, my mother said, "It doesn't look like nothing to me." She shifted through the pieces of my jewelry.

Just a little while ago, I'd been so excited about making all of these—especially when everyone really liked them. But I hadn't made a new piece in a couple of months. I guess my mind had been on so many other things.

"This is my favorite," my mom said, picking up the long chain that Diamond liked, too. I swear, there were so many times when I thought Diamond was more related to my mom than I was.

My mom really liked Diamond; I could see it in her eyes when she looked at her. And then there were the times when Diamond would come over and she and my mom would bond by looking through magazines before my mother would send her home with a whole truckload.

So many of those times I felt invisible in my own house, but I knew my mom wasn't trying to hurt my feelings. She couldn't help it. That was just the way she felt about me. And with all the stupid things I'd done, I felt the same way about myself right now.

"That's the one Diamond likes," I told my mother. "I'm picking out pieces to give to them to wear in San Francisco."

"Ah . . . then you've heard the good news."

I nodded. "Yeah, they told me in school today."

"Isn't that great?" my mother said. "They'll win in San Francisco this weekend, and then you'll be ready to join them in New York."

Again, I just nodded.

My mom tilted her head. "You don't seem happy."

"I am. I'm glad I didn't mess up the whole thing for them. I just messed it up for me."

"None of this was your fault, India."

She was just saying that to make me feel better, but she couldn't say anything to make me stop feeling stupid.

"You know," my mother began, and now her voice sounded softer and sadder, "I saw Dr. Yee today."

"Did I do something wrong?"

"No, sweetheart. Why would you think that?"

I shrugged. "'Cause I seem to do a lot of wrong things these days."

"That's not true."

"Yes, it is. Because of me, the Divine Divas almost didn't get to go to San Francisco. And because of me, I can't go." I stopped and looked at my mom. "And because of me, you're sad all the time."

"Honey, I'm not sad all the time, and when I am, it's not because of you."

No matter what she said, I knew the truth. My mother used to be so happy, almost singing when she talked about her charities and her modeling. But now, she hardly smiled, and she spent most of her time watching me. It didn't take a big brain to figure out whose fault this was.

"It's not you," she repeated. She put her head down a little and just looked at my jewelry box. "Dr. Yee wanted to see me to talk about a few things."

Okay, now see—this was going to be bad, because my mother wouldn't even look at me.

When she finally looked up, her eyes were filled with water, like she was about to cry. She looked that way a lot these days.

"I can tell you," Tova said, "that none of this is your fault." Then she did what I did when I had a hard time saying something. She took a deep breath. "Dr. Yee told me something today that was very interesting. Have you ever heard of genetic predisposition?"

I shook my head. That sounded like something out of a sci-fi movie.

"Well, genetic predisposition simply means that someone has something in them that makes them do a certain thing. Many times, it's not because they want to do it, there's just something inside of them that guides them that way."

It must've been the look on my face—like I didn't have a clue—that made my mom keep going.

"You know how you're always talking about Veronique being such a good singer and a good musician without taking any lessons?"

"Uh-huh. She can play that keyboard like Alicia Keys, but nobody taught Veronique."

"But you said her father was a musician, right?"

"Yeah, at least that's what she thinks. But she doesn't know a lot about him."

"It doesn't matter if she knows him or not—when she was born, her father's talent was passed down to her. It's in her genes. It's in her blood."

I was starting to get it. "I've heard people say that before—in her blood."

"Well . . ." My mother bit her lip before she said, "For you and purging—that may have been in your blood."

This did not make any kind of sense to me. I understood it with Veronique because that was her gift. But throwing up—how could that be in my blood? That wasn't any kind of talent.

"Dr. Yee says that all the research hasn't been done on this, but one thing many doctors seem to think is that eating disorders run in families."

Oh, okay. I got that. Jill *was* the one who told me how to get rid of food. And she was my family.

Then the shocker. "When I was younger, I used to throw up, too."

My eyes were way wide.

"It was something that started when I was modeling. In those days, everyone was doing it. But even afterwards, I had a hard time stopping." She paused for a minute. "I didn't want to stop. I wanted to do everything I could to stay skinny. I hardly ate, and when I did, I would throw up."

Now my mouth was open as wide as my eyes. Jill had mentioned that our mothers probably purged when they were younger, but there was no way I could have ever imagined Tova doing anything like that. I couldn't picture her leaning over a toilet!

"So, your purging—it may have started with me." When tears started coming out of her eyes, I felt bad all over again. "And," she kept on, "I feel like I let you down."

"No, you didn't."

"I did. I should have seen the signs. And I wish to God that I had. But I didn't. I don't know if it's because I didn't want to see them, or what." She took my hand. "But it will never happen again. I will never let you down. Not anymore."

I hugged my mother tighter than I had ever held her before.

When she pulled away from me, she said, "We're going to talk to Dr. Yee more about this tomorrow. She'll help you understand it better, okay?"

I nodded.

"But there is one thing, India. You're going to have to take responsibility, too. You're going to have to fight like heck to get over this. That's the only way I was able to beat it. I stopped and focused on being healthy. And that's the only way it will work for you." She took my hands and looked straight into my eyes. "I'm going to help you, because you are what's most important in my life."

I just looked back at her.

Her eyes got kind of narrow when she asked me, "Do you believe me?"

I wanted to, I wanted to so bad.

"I love you, your father loves you, and we're going to help you with this all the way."

Slowly, I nodded.

"Okay." My mom took a deep breath. "Enough of all this crying and sadness. I think we need to do something to celebrate you getting better."

I hoped she didn't want to go shopping—I didn't feel like doing that. And going to a restaurant—I really didn't want to do that either.

My mom pulled a folder from her jacket pocket. "How about this for a celebration?"

It didn't take me more than a second to figure out what this was—a plane ticket. My hands were shaking as I opened it up, even though I had already guessed where the plane was going—to San Francisco. The ticket said that I was leaving Friday. I wondered if I was on the same flight as my best friends.

"Oh, Tova," I said, hugging her. "I'm going to San Francisco?" I couldn't believe it.

"Yes, you're going, and your dad and I are going, too. We're all still part of the Divine Divas."

"That's so awesome."

My mother pulled back and looked at me. "It's been a little while since I've seen a smile like that," she said. "Give it to me again."

I grinned, and she did, too.

"Well, let me start getting dinner ready. Wanna come with me and help?" She reached out her hand and pulled me from the bed.

I followed my mother from my bedroom, not because I wanted to cook or anything, but because I didn't want this time with her to end. This had been the best talk I ever had with her. It wasn't the ticket to San Francisco, although that was way cool. It was that today was the first day in my entire life that I felt like my mom really understood me. She used to do what I was doing. She used to feel what I'd been feeling. She got me. I couldn't remember when I'd ever felt this good.

When we got to the kitchen, my mom said, "India, there's one more thing."

"Yes, Tova."

She still waited a couple of seconds before she said, "I made a huge mistake years ago. I thought that it would be cool and cute and different to have you call me Tova. It had nothing to do with how much I loved you. I've always loved you.

"But I think I missed out on a lot. On all of those years of hearing you calling me that wonderful name. So, do you think . . . can you . . . I'd rather hear you call me Mom from now on."

I had a blank look on my face, because at first, I couldn't figure out what she was talking about. Did she really want everyone to know that she was my mother?

My mom started talking faster. "If you don't want to, you don't have to . . . I was just hoping . . ."

I smiled.

"Plus, I want everyone to always know that you're my daughter."

Now that part made me feel way, way good. "Okay . . . Mom."

She smiled, put her arms around me, and we walked into the kitchen together.

chapter 27

My dad held my hand just as the plane floated right into the clouds.

"Are you excited, sweetheart?"

I was grinning big time when I nodded. "This is almost as good as getting on the stage and singing."

"Don't go getting any big ideas, because that is not going to happen, got that?" He had a smile on his face, but not in his voice.

"I know." My dad had been telling me that over and over ever since he and my mom bought these tickets for San Francisco. I guess he didn't want me to think one surprise was going to lead to another—I was definitely not getting on that stage.

But even though I wanted to sing real bad, I was cool with this. At least I'd be with my BFFs, and I'd still feel like I was one of the Divine Divas.

"As soon as Dr. Gerard releases you, you can go back to singing and dancing and being the diva that you are." My dad laughed and squeezed my fingers. And I squeezed him back. I loved holding his hands. Like when I hugged him, holding his hand made me feel like I was holding onto a big ole teddy bear.

"You know that you're special."

I nodded. "Sometimes I still have a hard time believing it, but Dr. Yee said that I have to start seeing myself like that. And Pastor Ford said that, too. She said that God thought that I was a star."

"Pastor's right about that. God knows you're a star, and your mother and I do, too."

I leaned forward a little and peeked across the aisle. My mother sat right across from us, but her seat was already back and her eyes were closed. She might have been sleeping, but she was kinda smiling, too. Things were definitely better at our house.

"India, I need to ask you something."

Uh-oh. Just when I thought this whole trip was going to be about fun, my dad was sounding all serious.

"Why didn't you come to me? Don't you know that you can talk to me about anything?"

Even though I'd been seeing Dr. Yee for two weeks now, this was the first time my dad was talking to me—without my mom or Dr. Yee—about what had happened. I guess he'd needed some time to figure out what to say.

I shrugged. "I never thought about talking to you or anyone because I didn't know how to explain that I was feeling bad. It was like it was real, real deep inside and I didn't understand it enough to talk about it."

My dad nodded like I was making sense.

So I kept going. "I didn't want to just say that I felt bad because I was fat. That sounded stupid to me."

"But you were never fat."

Okay, now see—he was just being my daddy, 'cause he knew I was fat. But I was starting to be okay with the way I used to look. As long as I never looked like that again.

"I guess I just didn't know what to say."

"That's a very grown-up understanding of it, but it's also mature to share your feelings with people who love and care about you."

"That's what Dr. Yee says."

"I hope you know my door is always open to you. No matter what you want to talk about. And my heart is open to you. My heart and your mother's, too."

Okay, he was getting way mushy and I didn't want to cry. I wanted to stay on the happy side.

"India, I hope you know that you are worthy no matter what is going on in your life."

I guess this was going to be one of those long Daddy talks. But I didn't mind it today. I had really wanted to talk to my dad about what had happened, and I didn't have to worry about him talking too long, because the flight from Los Angeles to San Francisco was about an hour.

"Here's the thing, India," he continued. "I love you with all my heart."

I believed that.

"And your mom loves you, too."

My mom had been telling me that a lot these days. I guess she had always shown me, but hearing her say it made me really believe it now.

"But no matter what anyone else says about you or does to you, you've got to find a way to love yourself."

I bit the corner of my lip. "I always hear people saying that you have to love yourself. But how do you do that?"

My dad shook his head a little bit, like he was really thinking. "I can't say there's an exact formula, but you've got to look at yourself and see all of the wonderful things you have to offer."

I couldn't think of a single thing I had to offer anyone.

"Your grandmother taught me not only how to appreciate what I had to offer, but how to make sure I was offering my gifts and talents to other people.

"I was just ten years old when my mother would make me write down at least one thing I'd done that day for someone else. At first, I couldn't think of anything, but then, not only did I start seeing what I was doing, but I began to look for ways to help people. It didn't matter if I smiled at someone who looked kind of sad that day, or if I helped a neighbor with her groceries." My dad crossed his legs and sat back like he was settling in for a long talk. "I gotta tell you, when I read back over that list at the end of the week, I felt pretty good about myself."

Wow. That was cool, but what was even better was that my dad was talking about when he was a boy. I loved hearing his stories, especially since my mom never talked about when she was a kid—she only talked about her modeling.

"I think I'm gonna try that, Daddy. And I'm gonna tell Diamond, Vee, and Aaliyah, too."

My dad smiled so wide, like he was proud that he'd told me something that I wanted to tell my friends. "That would be a good thing." Then he turned all serious again. "But I think the best way to learn how to love yourself is to realize that you're God's creation, and He didn't make a mistake. Every curve He put on your body, every line He put on your face—the size of your feet, the color of your skin, the length of your hair—all of that came from God. And He knew what He was doing the whole time.

"I kinda figure," Daddy said, "that if God made it, He loves it. And if He loves it, who am I to not love it?"

I went over in my head a couple of times what my dad just said. Tova had given me that equation about food and hips when I was a little girl. But I liked this equation from my dad way better: If God made it, He loves it, and if He loves it, then I need to love it, too.

I was going to make that my screen saver on my computer so that I could look at it every day.

"Thanks, Daddy."

"You're welcome, baby girl." He put his arms around me, and I lay my head on his chest.

That might not have been one of the longest Daddy talks, but I had to say, it was a good one. I was way happy right about then and couldn't wait to get to San Francisco. I knew the Divine Divas were going to tear up the stage, and then I would be back with them when we got ready to take over New York City!

chapter 28

I could hardly sit still in my seat.

The Civic Center was filled, just like the Kodak Theatre had been. And the crowd was buzzing—the air just felt like excitement.

But there was not a single person in there more excited than me.

I'd gone to the final rehearsal last night that had been held right here at the Civic Center. I'd stood on that big ole stage, looked out at all of those seats, and wished again that I was going to be doing my thing with my BFFs.

Last night, the Divine Divas had sounded totally awesome to me. Really, they'd even sounded better than we had when we'd won in Los Angeles. And then I'd had to push away that thought that had come to my mind—that they sounded better because I wasn't with them.

Dr. Yee was teaching me the difference between the positive thoughts that built you up and negative thoughts that tore you down. She was teaching me how to listen to what I said in my mind, and I couldn't believe how many negative thoughts I had about myself every day. But I was getting better—now that I knew that what you said to yourself inside was as important as the words you said out loud, I was really trying to focus on the positive.

And right now, that was all that I was doing—sitting on the edge of my seat and focusing on the positive. But it was easy to keep the negative thoughts about the Divine Divas away. I don't know what I'd been worried about, but Diamond was doing her thing. Listening to her last night, I'd almost wondered if she'd been taking singing lessons. Or maybe my hearing had just gotten clearer from being in the hospital. Or maybe she'd been in the hospital and had her vocal cords changed. I don't know what it was, but Diamond was holding it down. And of course, Veronique and Aaliyah were on point, too. No worries. My BFFs were fierce!

The lights dimmed, then we heard, from behind the curtain, "Good evening, ladies and gentlemen!" as Yolanda Adams, wearing a long golden dress and a matching head wrap, stepped onto the stage.

It sounded like a lion's roar the way the crowd cheered for her.

Not many people in the audience knew that Yolanda was going to be the mistress of ceremonies. But we did. She'd been at the rehearsals last night, and my friends and I had almost died when we'd met her backstage. Even Aaliyah, who was *never* impressed with anybody, had almost fallen out when Yolanda had shaken her hand.

Yolanda made a couple of jokes about how she would have never been able to compete against the talent that was here tonight. Even though everybody laughed, we all knew that was a straight lie. Please! Nobody could blow like Yolanda.

I guess what she said was just part of trying to get the crowd comfortable and relaxed, but there was nothing that she could say to make me sit back in my seat.

"Are you ready to get started?" she finally asked.

The applause was even louder this time; I was sure most of the noise was coming from me.

"Okay, then, let's bring out the first of the five groups tonight. First up, we have . . . the Divine Divas! Give it up, ladies and gentlemen."

Oh, my goodness! I didn't know my girls were going to be up first. While everyone around us applauded politely, our group, including Pastor Ford, stood to our feet and roared. I cracked up when my father whistled . . . and Pastor Ford, too! I couldn't believe a lady—and a preacher—could whistle loud like that. I was going to have to ask her to teach me how to do it.

"How's everybody out there?" Diamond said into her headset. "Before we begin, my crew and I just want to give a shout out to someone so special to us. She's supposed to be standing on this stage, but she can't tonight. But she's up here with us in spirit, and what's best, she's in the audience. So, to our sister, India, this one's for you!"

Oh my God! I didn't know they were going to do that. I stood up and waved, and again, the whole crew from our church clapped.

I wasn't sure that Diamond, Veronique, and Aaliyah could see me—I remembered that at the Kodak I couldn't see a thing in the crowd. But just the fact that they would say that about me made me want to cry.

But I didn't want any tears blocking my eyes from seeing everything, so I just shook them away, sat back down, and waited for my girls to bring it.

Diamond started off with, "Don't stop the music!"

She held that note and then Veronique and Aaliyah joined in.

"We just want to dance!"

They were stepping and singing and looking so good. It was funny, last time we'd worn special outfits that one of my mom's designers had made. But tonight, they just had on the jeans we'd all picked out and baby-tees (in different colors) with DIVINE DIVA written in silver on the front. And they still looked as if a designer had dressed them.

What was best was that I was wearing the exact same outfit—in a size eight. My mom had taken my jeans to a tailor to have them taken in. So even though I wasn't on stage, I felt like I was rocking with my girls.

Diamond was laying it down! She was singing like she'd never sung before. She was singing as if she might never sing again. Sybil always said that on the stage we had to put it all out there until you had nothing left. I never really understood that until I watched Diamond tonight.

It wasn't until Diamond hit that last note and Veronique and Aaliyah joined in with the harmony that I realized I hadn't been breathing.

There was just a moment of silence, and then I jumped up and cheered like I never had before. I didn't know if anyone around me was clapping. Didn't matter to me. My BFFs had just sang their butts off, and I was so proud.

"Whew!" Yolanda said when she came back onto the stage. "Did you hear those young sistahs?" She shook her head. "They weren't singing, they were sanging!" she kidded. "So, let's hear it once again for the Divine Divas!"

People clapped, and now I let the tears come out of my eyes. But it was a happy, happy cry, because my best friends had been fab-u-lous.

I wanted so bad to go backstage, but here in San Francisco, they said no one besides the performers could be back there until the end of the show.

The group after the Divine Divas was the Faithful Five, the girls and guys who hadn't been very nice to us in Los Angeles. Even though I didn't want to admit it, they sounded pretty good as they sang a hip-hop version of "Jesus Loves Me." I don't know why they kept picking those old-school songs. This was supposed to be a young competition. But even though their song was tired, they did sound good. Maybe it was the harmony that you got combining males and females—I don't know. Not that it mattered, because they were nowhere near my sisters. The Divine Divas were way, way better.

By the time the last group ran off the stage almost an hour later, I was convinced. My BFFs were better than all of the other four groups combined. It was such a wrap—we had won for sure!

I was already planning the trip to New York in my head. Since it was all the way across country, I hoped our parents let us go for a week. I couldn't wait to do some shopping. I kinda laughed inside. Even though I wasn't purging, I still wanted to go shopping. I might be a size six by then—the healthy way, of course.

When Yolanda Adams brought all of the groups back onto the stage, I was almost falling off my seat—that's how close to the edge I was sitting. I was just getting ready to jump straight into the air the moment they announced the Divine Divas as winners.

"Ladies and gentlemen, please give a hand to all of our groups. Aren't they all winners?"

As all five groups smiled and bowed, I didn't take my eyes off the Divine Divas. Diamond and Veronique and Aaliyah were holding hands and smiling, but they looked a little scared, like they weren't sure.

I wanted to laugh. It was so different sitting in the audience. You could just hear the difference in the groups, and you could tell who'd won. My BFFs didn't have a thing to worry about.

Then Roberto Hamilton, the president of Glory 2 God Productions, came on stage to announce the winner.

"Like Yolanda said, aren't they all winners?"

Oh God! I thought. Why did they have to drag this out? Couldn't they just get this over with and tell everyone that the Divine Divas had won?

My legs were shaking and my hands were sweaty, like I was nervous or something. But it really wasn't nervousness. It was more of just wanting to get this over.

"Now, let's get on with this," Roberto said.

Finally!

"And the state champions, who will go on to compete with ten other groups in New York City, are . . ."

Why was he dragging this out?

"The Faithful Five!"

What?

A cheer came from the crowd, but not from anyone in the Hope Chapel crew. I looked at my BFFs on the stage, and they were as shocked as I was.

Something had gone way wrong. Hadn't Mr. Hamilton heard the Divine Divas sing? Maybe he had come in late and missed their performance. Someone had to tell him that this was a major mistake.

I was just sitting still, staring at my friends as they slowly walked off the stage. I didn't move until my dad took my hand. It was a good thing he was holding onto me, because I don't think I would've been able to walk by myself.

Nobody said a word as we zigzagged through the crowd. We bumped into some people who were obviously fans of that group that won, because they were jumping up and down and cheering and crying. They were doing all the things that we were supposed to be doing.

I was still stunned when we walked into the room reserved for the Divine Divas, but as soon as I saw my friends, I let it all out. And so did they.

We hugged and cried, all of us in complete and total shock.

"I'm so sorry," Diamond said.

I sniffed. "Why are you sorry?"

"'Cause this is all my fault. I should've let Vee sing the lead," Diamond wailed. "Then we would've won."

Veronique was shaking her head no. Even though she wasn't crying hard like Diamond, I guess it was still kinda hard for her to speak.

"It wasn't your fault, Diamond," I said, even though I was crying hard. "It was mine. If I hadn't gotten sick, then you wouldn't have been distracted. I messed it all up!"

That was when I felt my dad's teddy bear arms all around me. I couldn't believe I was this sad. When I looked up, I saw Diamond and Aaliyah's fathers were holding them, too. And Pastor Ford had her arms around Veronique. That was good, because Veronique's mother hadn't been able to come to San Francisco. Even Sybil had some tears in her eyes.

"I need to say something to everyone," Pastor said.

We all stopped talking and kinda joined in a circle to listen to our pastor.

"First of all, girls, I am so proud of you. Your parents are proud of you. Sybil is proud of you. Everyone at Hope Chapel is proud of you."

Around us, the adults all nodded. But that wasn't really making me feel any better.

"Do you know how good you sounded out there?" she said. "You were . . . fierce!"

187

It was supposed to be a joke, and I guess it was funny. But it was just too hard to laugh right now.

"This was nobody's fault," Pastor Ford continued. "You went out there and did the best you could. And that's what makes you winners."

The adults nodded, but not one of my BFFs moved. I was just glad that my dad was holding me up.

"One thing I know is that God's got this. You never know what He has in store. You don't know His plans. But you know that His plans are better than anything you could have put together for yourself.

"Tonight when you all go home," Pastor Ford continued, and this time she looked directly at me and my BFFs, "I want you to look up a scripture—Jeremiah twenty-nine eleven. And I want you girls to write that verse down on an index card, memorize it, and say it over and over until it is part of you. And you will always know, you will always be able to say God's words back to Him whenever you have any doubts. Okay?"

We all nodded. None of us were crying anymore, but all of our sadness was still right there on our faces. I did feel a little better though—it was always like that with Pastor Ford. It was like she brought peace right into the room with her.

"I want to pray right now."

Everyone held hands, then bowed their heads. But I had a hard time listening. All I could think about was the hard work we'd put into this since September. We'd thought that we were going to go all the way—Diamond had convinced us of that.

But now I didn't have a clue what was going to happen to us. Even though we didn't win, maybe we could still be the Divine Divas. We could sing at church, and at parties, and different things like that.

But even as I had that thought, I knew that wouldn't fly.

Diamond wouldn't go for that. Her plans had been big—to make us all super-stars. I had to remember to tell her what Pastor had told me about stars.

"Amen," I heard everyone say.

Pastor Ford said, "The last thing I want to say to you girls is that when one door closes, God always opens up another. So no matter what, just stay prepared. Be ready for all the great things He has for you."

Then Pastor kissed each one of us before she left the room. Her plane was leaving earlier than ours because we had planned to stay in San Francisco and celebrate with dinner on Fisherman's Wharf. But I didn't feel like celebrating, and I could tell that my BFFs weren't feeling that anymore either. It was time for us to just go home.

"Well, are you ladies ready for dinner?" Mr. Heber, Aaliyah's father, said.

I couldn't believe he was asking us that. We all shook our heads.

But then Mr. Heber continued. "Remember what Pastor said. If you're stars, if you're divas, then you hold your heads up and move on." He looked straight into our eyes when he said, "Ladies, there is still a lot to celebrate. Do you know how many young ladies in this world would love to be wearing your shoes right now? Never forget your blessings."

"Yes," every parent in that room agreed.

I guess we didn't have a choice. Our parents were going to make this into a happy occasion no matter what.

As the adults walked out of the room, Diamond grabbed my hand, pulled me back, and motioned for Veronique and Aaliyah to come back, too.

When it was just the four of us in the room, Diamond said, "We're still the Divine Divas, and no matter what, we shouldn't give up."

189

I was shocked to hear her say that. I didn't think Diamond would want anything to do with this anymore.

"So what are we gonna do?" I asked.

Diamond shook her head. "I don't know, but I believe Pastor. Something good is going to come out of this."

At first, Veronique looked like she thought Diamond was crazy, but then she said, "I think so, too. I think we really need to pray about it."

Diamond nodded. "That'll work. 'Cause I'm telling you, we're born to be stars, and I'm never giving up on that."

I nodded, only because I knew that's what Diamond wanted me to do. But I couldn't even think of one thing we could do to turn this around.

"I think praying is a good thing," Aaliyah jumped in. "We'll just pray and then kiss it up to God."

"Kiss it up to God?" the three of us said at the same time.

"Yeah, like this." Aaliyah pressed her fingers to her lips, kissed them, and then blew the kiss up to the sky, like she was sending a kiss to heaven.

It was just like when I was a little girl, and if I dropped a piece of candy on the ground and I still wanted to eat it, I would kiss it up to God.

Aaliyah said, "Let's kiss the Divine Divas up to God and we'll see what He can do."

I'm not sure if Diamond and Veronique got this—I know I didn't. On the real, it was sounding a little crazy to me. But one thing I did notice as we stood in our little circle—instead of all the sadness that was on our faces just a little while ago, all I saw now was hope.

Aaliyah said, "We should all say our own little prayer to ourselves, and then on the count of three, we'll kiss it up to God together."

We all nodded and bowed our heads.

Inside, I prayed for God's best for the Divine Divas, and then I decided to add in a little bit extra for me. I prayed that God would really help me not to binge and purge again. And that He would help me to be a good weight where I could be proud to look in the mirror. I prayed that I would get well, and that my mother would, too.

"Okay, on the count of three," Aaliyah said. "One, two, three. . . ."

We all kissed our fingertips, then raised our hands in the air.

I couldn't figure out why, but that felt really good. And as I stood there in the quiet with my friends who were really my sisters, I had a feeling that nothing but good things were going to come out of this. I had a feeling that something I always heard the adults say would be true for us—that prayer changes things.

Our prayers were going to change a lot of things, and now I couldn't even wait to see what was going to happen next.

Readers Group Guide

Summary

Diamond, India, Veronique, and Aaliyah are fifteen-year-old high school sophomores who have been best friends since childhood. After forming a singing group, the Divine Divas, in order to enter a gospel talent search and winning a preliminary contest, the girls must prepare for the next round in San Francisco. This second part of the Divas' story is seen through the eyes of India, who doesn't feel like she fits in anywhere. She is the daughter of a former model, though overweight herself, and she's racially mixed. India's distress and plummeting self-esteem get overshadowed by the Divas' excitement over their competition, and her feelings of invisibility grow stronger. She is overjoyed to learn what she thinks is a secret, beginning a cycle of binging and purging that causes her to lose weight rapidly. At first, India and everyone around her is impressed by her shrinking size. But by the time India's closest friends and family realize how bad things are, India is in the hospital, and the chance to continue in the gospel talent search is in jeopardy.

Discussion Points

1. In the opening of the novel, India says, "This world wasn't made for me." What exactly makes India feel so different and alone? Have you ever felt this way, and if so, how did you deal with it?

2. From the very beginning of this novel, India feels neglected by her friends. Do you think this is true? Are India's feelings based on reality or are they self-imposed? Give examples from the novel to support your opinion.

3. If you've read the first novel in this series, how do you think the Divas have been changed by their experiences? In what ways do you see them responding differently to situations?

4. India overhears her parents arguing about her weight problem. From the conversation, it is clear that Tova wants to get India some kind of stomach surgery in order to help her lose weight, while India's father is firmly against this plan. Why do you think he says no? How do you feel about surgery as a "quick fix" to physical problems? When might such surgery be useful and "okay"?

5. Tova says that she wants to give India self-esteem and confidence by getting her the surgery she thinks she needs to be thin. Does thin equal confident? How does this equation seem supported by the events of this novel as experienced by India? What do you think about this idea?

6. On page 52, Jill says, "It can't be bad if it's on the 'Net." Do you think this is true? How does the availability of infor-

mation in today's high-tech world affect how people perceive its value? When you surf the internet, how do you evaluate what you are seeing?

7. India is thrilled to discover Jill's "secret" for losing weight quickly. But while she seems to believe it's okay to vomit up her meals, she also instinctively knows that she will get into trouble if anyone finds out. What is it that keeps India from telling anyone about her great new weight-loss plan? What does her behavior reveal? What other reasons might there be for keeping such a secret?

8. The journalist Nicolette brings up the issue of models and eating disorders to Tova, who dismisses the topic as being somewhat exaggerated. How big of a problem do you think eating disorders really are in today's world? Give examples of people being unaware of how their words affect others, like Nicolette's comment to India about losing her "baby fat."

9. On page 140, Pastor Ford tells India that she is a star for God. What does her advice tell you about your source of self-worth and how it affects your choices? How does the way in which you determine your own value affect how you perceive yourself versus the reality? How did it affect India?

10. When Pastor Ford points out to India that she is defining herself by her weight, India wonders, "How else was I supposed to define myself?" (page 139). Later, Dr. Yee asks India, "Tell me about yourself," a request that India finds difficult to answer. Why is it so hard for her to answer Dr. Yee? How do *you* define yourself?

11. When India's bulimia is exposed, Tova is distraught. She thought she was just helping her daughter by encouraging her to lose weight; India took her mother's advice as proof that Tova did not really like her because she was fat. Describe some of the things that Tova does that contribute to India's low self-esteem. What might she have done differently? What other ways are there to be supportive of someone who is trying to change?

12. On page 179, India's father shares with her a task his mother made him perform in childhood: every day, he had to write down one thing that he did for someone else. He tells India that, at the end of the week, seeing this list made him feel good about himself. Do you think it would work to help girls like India feel better about their bodies? Why or why not?

Enhance Your Book Club Experience

1. Once she begins therapy for her eating disorder and general self-esteem issues, India becomes more aware of all the negative things she says to herself throughout the day. What does your inner dialogue sound like? For one day, write down all of the things you say to yourself and, in the evening, make a tally of how many thoughts are positive and how many are negative. Then, for one day, try changing every negative thought into a positive one and see how it makes you feel.

2. At the end of the novel, the Divas are sad to lose their competition yet still feel positive about their future as a singing group. They "kiss it up to God" and remind them-

selves that when God closes one door, he opens another. At your next book club meeting, share with your fellow members a story about a time when this saying held true for you.

3.   Take some time to visit and browse the official Divas' websites at www.thedivinedivas.com and www.myspace.com/divinedivaseries_2008. You can also read the author's blog at www.myspace.com/victoriachristophermurray. Come to your next book club meeting prepared to discuss how the internet allows authors to bring the world of their novels to life, and how this author's personal thoughts has or hasn't affected your experience reading her novels.

Questions for the Author

Q. Before the Divas, you primarily concerned yourself with adult characters. What led to your decision to write a young-adult series?

A. I received so many emails from young readers who were enjoying my books that I decided I needed to write a story for them. Additionally, I noticed that many teenagers were reading books that were written for adults because there wasn't enough material on the market for them. So the Divine Divas were born.

Q. How is it different to write for a teen audience versus an adult audience? Do you have a preference?

A. I still feel more comfortable writing for adults, but writing about these four divas has been more fun! I write the teen characters in first person, so that I can really get into their heads, while I keep my adult novels in third person.

Q. Each novel in the Divas series is told from the point of view of a different girl. What are some of the challenges writing about the same "world" using such different voices and perspectives? What does this technique allow you to do that you otherwise couldn't?

A. I don't find it a challenge writing from these four perspectives at all! It's wonderful because it's the same world, but seen so differently by each girl. This gives me a chance to show that's how it is in real life. So many people think the world is about them. They expect people to believe what they believe, to make the same decisions they would make. Writing this series in this manner allows me to show that people may see the same things and draw very different conclusions.

Q. Tell us what came first: the characters, or the concept?

A. I think the concept of four girls who wanted to sing came first. And then I developed characters to tell that story. That's the same process for my adult novels, too.

Q. *Divas: India* is your second novel in this series. What tricks do you use to maintain the characters' growth and the storylines from one book to the next? Are there any techniques you use in each book to refresh readers' memories about what happened in the previous installment?

A. Wow—I wish I had some tricks! But I don't have any at all. I just write what's in my heart. I do—through memory or short flashbacks—remind readers what happened in the previous book. I do this so that if someone didn't read the first book, they won't feel lost. It's a technique that I use in my adult novels as well. Even though the books are connected, someone can pick up any book and still enjoy the characters, the story, and the experience.

Q. The four Divas are so different, yet they are as tight as sisters! As their creator, what would you say really bonds them to one another? Is it simply that they have been friends since childhood? Is it something else they share in common?

A. My divas share a couple of things. First, they have been friends since childhood. Next, none of them have any biological sisters, so they've shared good times and bad times and secrets with each other for many years. But each of them has a secret that she's never shared with any of the others.

Q. You write so convincingly from the point of view of teenagers. Where do you find your inspiration? What kind of research do you do for each novel to maintain the authenticity of your teenage characters?

A. My iPod is now filled with TV shows geared toward teenagers! I have *Baldwin Hills* and *Lincoln Heights* and *Gossip Girl*. I don't watch these shows to get ideas—I have more than enough of those on my own. But I watch the shows to hear the language, check out the body movements, and, most important, see what the ladies are wearing!

Q. One of the biggest internet safety concerns recently has been the rocketing growth of MySpace and the op-

portunity it creates for young people, especially teens, to be taken advantage of. Yet you have a successful presence on MySpace yourself, and a unique twist—a page written by the Divas themselves! What do you have to say about how such technologies can be both a curse and a blessing? What words of wisdom can you offer teens to help them benefit from the unlimited possibilities of the internet instead of being harmed by it?

A. Interesting that you would ask me this—my third book, *The Divas: Veronique,* is about the internet and the dangers that exist with it. The internet can be a wonderful tool when used properly. But it can be just as dangerous, and I hope the next book shows teens how to use the internet effectively and safely.

Q. As a Christian and an artist, what role does God play in your creative process?

A. God plays the most important part, not only in the creative process, but in every part of my life. I always say that being a Christian is not an adjective, it's a verb. It's what I do. So in every part of my thinking, God is involved. He's not compartmentalized in my life; He's in every part, every sentence, every story that I write. He's part of every day, every hour, every minute that I live.

Q. India often seems to find the most negative interpretation of what could just as easily be an innocent comment or event. How often do you think our perceptions differ from reality? Is this a problem that you see as primarily plaguing teen girls?

A. I think that is a self-esteem problem and has nothing to do with age or gender. If you don't feel good about yourself, you will see something negative in everything someone does and everything someone says.

Q. Beyond the fact that the girls are competing in a gospel talent search contest, the role of their Christian faith is expressed very subtly throughout the novel. Was this a conscious choice on your part, and if so, why?

A. This is an interesting question—I think people read things in my book that I didn't put in there purposefully. I don't sit down and plan things—I don't say, "Okay, what is my subtle message?" I just write what's in my heart. As I said before, my faith is important to me and it has to show up in my writing. But I'm not, and none of these girls are, religious fanatics. Their faith is just a normal part of their everyday lives. That's probably why it seems to be so subtle.

If you enjoyed *The Divas: India*, don't miss

The Divas: Veronique

Coming soon from Pocket Books

Turn the page for a sneak preview . . .

"Did you look at my page?" I asked Diamond, the moment I walked into her bedroom.

She closed the door. We weren't alone in the house this time, although I didn't think their housekeeper, Carmen, was going to give us any trouble. Whenever I said hello to her, all Carmen did was smile.

"No, I didn't look at your page. Why would I do that?" Diamond answered. "This is your thing."

"I thought you would check on it for me—at least over the weekend." I moved right to the computer, clicked it on, and after a minute, signed onto the internet.

I was so excited, but when I looked over my shoulder, Diamond was sitting on her bed, texting somebody. As if finding my father was all about nothing.

I couldn't blame my sistah for not feelin' this like I was. I mean, she had her father; she couldn't understand.

My fingers were trembling as I opened my page. And then, I screamed.

"What?" Diamond jumped off her bed and, with one hop, was looking over my shoulder.

"I got messages!" I clicked on the message icon. Thirteen! I couldn't believe it.

Last week, after we couldn't find a listing for Pierre Garrett in New York City, Diamond and I designed my personal page. It had taken us two days, but I'd posted my picture and profile saying I was looking for my father, Pierre Garrett, who lived in New York.

"Should we put your dad's name on here?" Diamond had asked. "We don't want any imposters."

"No worries," I said, figuring I needed to play it straight. "I'll be able to spot a fake a mile away."

"How?"

I didn't bother to answer. And even though she wasn't sure, I left my dad's name right up there. I would never be able to explain it to Diamond, but just like she knew her father, I would know mine. A fake would never get by me. Trust and know.

And now today, I had messages! Could one of these be from my father?

My hands were still shaking when I clicked on the first message—from Cool Hand Luke. Interesting name. Especially for a father.

"Hey," Diamond said the moment the message came on the screen. "He's hot."

I rolled my eyes. I didn't care not one single solitary bit what this guy looked like. And I cared even less when he talked about "hookin' up with a cutie like me." Not only was this boy not my father, could he even read? I hadn't said anything about hooking up.

"Yeah, he's a major cutie," Diamond said.

"Can we just focus, please?"

"I am!" She was telling the truth. She was focused, almost drooling over this guy's picture.

She dragged a chair over to the desk. "Let's see what else you got."

I should've been grateful to Cool Hand Luke. At least he made my sistah throw down her phone and give me some backup.

The next four messages were just like Luke's. From boys who wanted me to send more pictures to the ones who wanted my digits. Then there were the ones who wanted to hook up in person. Like I would do something dumb like that.

I was getting pretty sick of it. But Diamond wasn't.

"Some of these boys are major cute," Diamond said. "Maybe I should make a page."

"I thought your mom wouldn't let you have one."

She waved her hand in the air. "When have you known me to listen to the judge?" Diamond asked. "And anyway, you have a page."

"I'm not her daughter."

"You think the judge is going to see the difference when she finds out about this?" Diamond laughed.

"She's not going to find out, right?" I said and clicked on another message. In two seconds flat, Diamond had stopped laughing. Both of our mouths were open wide as we read this one.

After awhile, Diamond said, "Eeewww! Gross! I told you this site was full of perverts!"

All I did was hit the delete button. I didn't even want to think about the nasty things that guy had said. But a minute later, I was hitting the delete button again. And then, again.

"See! I told you this wasn't going to work!"

I just kept deleting messages, trying really hard not to listen to Diamond. But truth—she was right. All of those messages and not one of them had anything to do with my father.

Diamond pushed her chair back from the desk. "We need to forget about this," she said as I turned off the computer. "It's never going to work." She flopped onto her bed and grabbed her Sidekick again.

I was beginning to think that Diamond was so right. There weren't a lot of things that made me cry, but I felt like this was going to be one of those crying times.

"Let's talk to my dad."

My eyes got all big. "No! I told you, this is a secret."

"Yeah, but searching the internet isn't going to work and my dad can help."

Diamond didn't even know that she was making it worse. The first thing she did when she had a problem was turn to her father. Couldn't she figure out that I wanted the same thing?

"I don't want your father in this, Diamond. I want to do it myself."

"But . . ."

"Come on; this is just the first day. I have to learn how to really use the internet."

But it was like Diamond didn't even hear me. "Well, if you don't want to talk to my dad, what about Mr. Heber? Top Cop can find anybody!"

Okay, sure, Mr. Heber was deputy chief of police, but how did Diamond think talking to Aaliyah's father was any better? I didn't need to be reminded that they both had their dads. And India had hers, too.

I said, "Let's stick with this for a little while, *please*? And if it doesn't work, I'll figure something else out."

Diamond shook her head.

"We promised each other! This is my secret and you said. . . ."

Diamond held up her hand. "Okay, okay. But . . ." She glared at me. "I'm not feelin' this."

"No worries. It's gonna work."

She sighed and grabbed her purse. "I hope so. You ready?"

I guess my sistah was ready to take me home. No prob—I was ready to go.

As I followed Diamond out of her bedroom, I was trying to figure out what I was going to do next. Because there was no way I was going to give up. Not now. Not ever.

Finding my father wasn't a choice; it was what I absolutely had to do.

I really need a cell phone, I thought as I ran up the stairs.

Then I would've called Big Mama and let her know that I was gonna be late. It was only ten minutes after six, but still, my grandmother hated when I wasn't there when she brought my brothers home. Most of the time, she stayed with us until Mama got off from work. But when she had something else to do, all she wanted was to drop off D'Andre and 'em and be on her way. I prayed this wasn't one of those drop-off and leave times.

I was all the way out of breath by the time I got to our apartment. I pushed the door open. "Hey, Big Mama."

"Your grandmother's not here."

I was shocked when I heard my Mama's voice and my heart was pounding even more as I walked toward the kitchen. Something big-time must've happened for my mother to be home from work so early.

"Hey, Mama." I dropped my backpack on the floor and waited to hear the bad news.

When she faced me with a smile, I breathed.

"Hey, baby." She pulled a pan filled with a big ole chicken out of the oven. "How was practice?"

I tried not to frown too much, but it was hard. My mother *never* asked anything about me. "Good." I was still trying to figure this out. The kitchen table was covered with all kinds of pots and bowls like my mom was cooking a big holiday dinner. But Thanksgiving and Christmas were a long ways away. What was my mother doing home on a work day?

"Are you okay?"

"Yeah, baby." Mama laughed. "I just decided to take the day off; take a little time for myself."

Okay, so maybe nothing was wrong on the outside, but something was definitely wrong with Mama on the inside. Why was she taking so much time off from work recently? In the two weeks since D'Wayne had been back, this was the third time Mama had taken off. Was she sick? Or maybe she was . . . no! I couldn't even think about her having another baby.

She said, "I thought it would be great to have a nice dinner. This'll be ready in a little while." She was so happy, it sounded like she was singing, when she was just talking.

I stared at her a little longer. She didn't look like she was pregnant. Now, I was happy, too. "You want me to help with anything?"

"What about your homework?"

Oh, Mama was in a good mood because she always wanted me to help, whether I had homework or not. "I have some words to study for French, but I can do that after dinner."

"Okay, make the salad. Wash your hands first."

I stood at the sink and listened as my mother hummed that new song from Zena, "It's Gonna Be All the Way Right."

The only time my mother was like this was on the days she got paid. That never lasted long because after she paid the bills, she went right back to her tired-sad mood.

I loved hearing her hum. This was how I wanted her to be all the time. After I found my father, this would be her life.

He would make so much money that Mama would never work again. She would stay home and cook and take care of us.

And she would never be tired. And never be sad. And would hum every day.

As I sliced up the tomatoes, I asked, "Mama, why did my father leave?"

She stopped humming, but she was still smiling as she stirred the rice in the pot. "Your father?"

I nodded.

"Are you asking because of what I said about D'Wayne and the boys the other day?"

I shook my head. Mama had no idea—I thought about my dad all the time. "I was just thinkin'. . . ."

"Your father didn't just get up and walk out, baby. We both agreed to separate because Pierre had other things he needed to do. He was dying to go to Europe."

Mama had told me that before. How my father wanted to hook up with his mother's side of the family.

She kept on, "He wanted to go to France and I wanted to stay here."

"But he didn't stay there long, right?"

"Nope, he was back in like three months."

"So, why didn't he come back here? Or why didn't you go to New York?"

"Because we both knew that we weren't supposed to be together. We'd made a mistake. Pierre didn't love me. He only married me because . . ."

Mama stopped. Mama always stopped when she got to that part of the story. But even though she never said anything else, I knew the rest because Big Mama had told me—Mama was pregnant when she and my dad got married. Big Mama had to sign the papers because Mama was only sixteen—the same age that Big Mama was when she got pregnant with her baby—my mother.

That's why Big Mama was always telling me that I had to break the curse. And now that I was only a couple of months away from being sixteen, Big Mama repeated that story and her warning every single solitary chance she got.

I said, "I just wish he had come back to L.A. so that I could see him all the time."

"He didn't like Los Angeles, baby. He came here for college," she said, telling me the same story again. "But then we got married and had you. He had to work, go to school. . . ." Mama's sad voice was back. "I know you miss him," she said softly. "But the way it turned out, it really was for the best."

How could my mother say that? The way we were living—this wasn't the best of anything.

Mama said, "Even though it didn't work out for your father and me, I always wanted you. I was happy I had you then and I'm happy I have you now."

Mama always told me that—I think she never wanted me to feel bad. And truth—it did make me feel all the way good.

Then Mama said something that she'd never said before, "Your father wanted you, too."

At first, I was shocked, but then I wondered, Why was I surprised? Of course my dad wanted me and loved me. He was probably looking for me right now.

"Do you ever think about Dad?" I asked.

"Dad?" Her eyebrows went up high on her forehead like she was surprised with the way I called him Dad. But that's who he was to me.

Mama said, "I don't think about him too much because it's been a long time since I heard anything from him. And for so many years, I've had D'Wayne." Her voice got all happy again.

Why did she have to go and mess up everything like that?

"D'Wayne has helped me move on," she said.

Move on? Move on to where? D'Wayne hadn't helped my mother do a single solitary thing.

It made me a little mad when Mama started humming again, this time that old song "Endless Love." As if she could only hum when she was thinking about D'Wayne.

But that was okay. Soon she'd be humming for my daddy. I was going to make sure of it.